They were withi
distance

Greg proved it by wrapping an arm around her waist and hauling her against his very hard, exceedingly fine chest. No mistaking signals this time. She didn't resist his embrace.

Her lips parted the moment they made contact with his. Before she quite realized what was happening, he'd backed her up and pinned her to the wall. But this wasn't a combat drill, and Greg wasn't her opponent. She welcomed his long, lean body into her arms and returned his hot, hungry kisses with equal fervor.

Seconds stretched into minutes. Corrine was in no hurry to come to her senses. For all her tough exterior, she was pure woman on the inside. Responding to Greg's male advances felt not only natural, it felt right. Groaning, he lowered his hands to cup her hips and fit her more snugly between him and the wall. She shifted, improving their alignment to bone-melting perfection.

Returning to civilian life had suddenly taken on a whole new meaning.

Dear Reader,

About two years ago I was meeting with my editor, and she said to me, "Why don't you write a book with twins?" Seeing as I'm the mother of twins, this struck me as a really good suggestion.

With so many servicemen and servicewomen returning home in recent months, I liked the idea of bringing Corrine, one of the four Sweetwater sisters, back to the ranch after an eight-year stint in the army. She'd been in charge of feeding thousands of soldiers. Feeding a couple hundred guests should be easy, right? I then considered what kind of man would be a good match for this type A, by-the-book former warrant officer. Why, a type B man, of course. And who's more laid-back than a professional fisherman? One with troublesome twin five-year-olds and a mischievous dog to boot. Greg Pfitser has just the right amount of chaos in his life to shake up Corrine's.

I hope you enjoy reading about the ensuing results. I certainly had a good time writing them and walking down memory lane as I recalled the many antics my own twins pulled on me over the years.

Warmest regards,

Cathy McDavid

P.S. I always enjoy hearing from readers. You can contact me at www.cathymcdavid.com.

Taking on Twins
CATHY McDAVID

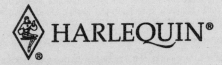

HARLEQUIN®

TORONTO • NEW YORK • LONDON
AMSTERDAM • PARIS • SYDNEY • HAMBURG
STOCKHOLM • ATHENS • TOKYO • MILAN • MADRID
PRAGUE • WARSAW • BUDAPEST • AUCKLAND

Recycling programs
for this product may
not exist in your area.

ISBN-13: 978-0-373-75298-0

TAKING ON TWINS

Copyright © 2010 by Cathy McDavid.

All rights reserved. Except for use in any review, the reproduction or
utilization of this work in whole or in part in any form by any electronic,
mechanical or other means, now known or hereafter invented, including
xerography, photocopying and recording, or in any information storage
or retrieval system, is forbidden without the written permission of the
publisher, Harlequin Enterprises Limited, 225 Duncan Mill Road,
Don Mills, Ontario, Canada M3B 3K9.

This is a work of fiction. Names, characters, places and incidents are
either the product of the author's imagination or are used fictitiously,
and any resemblance to actual persons, living or dead, business
establishments, events or locales is entirely coincidental.

This edition published by arrangement with Harlequin Books S.A.

® and TM are trademarks of the publisher. Trademarks indicated with
® are registered in the United States Patent and Trademark Office, the
Canadian Trade Marks Office and in other countries.

www.eHarlequin.com

Printed in U.S.A.

ABOUT THE AUTHOR

For the past eleven years Cathy McDavid has been juggling a family, a job and writing, and has been doing pretty well at it except for the cooking and housecleaning part. Mother of boy and girl teenage twins, she manages the near impossible by working every day with her husband of twenty years at their commercial construction company. They survive by not bringing work home and not bringing home to the office. A mutual love of all things Western also helps. Horses and ranch animals have been a part of Cathy's life since she moved to Arizona as a child and asked her mother for riding lessons. She can hardly remember a time when she couldn't walk outside and pet a soft, velvety nose (or beak or snout) whenever the mood struck. You can visit her Web site at www.cathymcdavid.com.

Books by Cathy McDavid

HARLEQUIN AMERICAN ROMANCE

1168—HIS ONLY WIFE
1197—THE FAMILY PLAN
1221—COWBOY DAD
1264—WAITING FOR BABY

Don't miss any of our special offers. Write to us at the following address for information on our newest releases.

Harlequin Reader Service
U.S.: 3010 Walden Ave., P.O. Box 1325, Buffalo, NY 14269
Canadian: P.O. Box 609, Fort Erie, Ont. L2A 5X3

To my brother John.
The most avid fisherman I know. Remember those
long summer days spent at Sabonis's pond?

Chapter One

"You can't quit, Pr—" Corrine Sweetwater started to say "Private" but caught herself an instant before the word slipped out.

She wasn't a warrant officer anymore, and the young man with tattoos covering his arms, neck and forehead wasn't her subordinate. Too bad. A few days on garbage detail might improve his attitude.

"The hell I can't." Danny or Donny or Johnny or whatever his name was stormed out of the kitchen.

Her assistant cook, Gerrie, removed a steaming pan of lasagna from the top rack of an oversize convection oven. Closing the door with her hip, she hummed "Another One Bites the Dust" by Queen.

Corrine had just lost her second dishwasher in as many weeks. Her third since arriving at Bear Creek Ranch, the guest resort owned by her family.

But who was counting?

Apparently Pat, the cook's helper and relief busgirl, was. "What's that make now? Three?"

In Corrine's opinion, Pat needed to get a hobby. "Have you cut up the salad greens?"

"Yes."

Corrine stood, waiting out of a habit she couldn't seem to break for a "ma'am" to follow that answer. It didn't come.

How long until she stopped expecting her subordinates—make that staff—to snap to attention when she entered the kitchen? Stopped thinking of her cousin, Jake Tucker, the manager of Bear Creek Ranch, as her commanding officer? Stopped demanding complete and unquestioning obedience from her dishwashers?

Seven weeks obviously wasn't long enough for her to adjust to civilian life.

"What are you going to do?" Gerrie asked, the barest hint of snideness in her voice.

Like the six, down from seven, coworkers busy at their various stations, Corrine's assistant cook had been employed here for a number of years. Their long-standing service to the Tucker family was probably the reason they hadn't followed Danny or Donny out the door. It certainly wasn't because they liked Corrine or, as Gerrie had put it when she didn't think Corrine was listening, her "anal retentive micromanaging."

"I'll figure something out." She finished wrapping the last of forty loaves of garlic bread in aluminum foil, and stacked it on a tray alongside the others. "Any of you interested in a little overtime?"

"Nope."

"Can't."

"Not tonight."

The excuses chimed one after another, sounding a lot like grade-schoolers' responses to attendance call.

"Fine."

"Figuring something out" would probably entail her working until midnight again—alone, unless she roped one of her sisters, parents or extended family into helping. They were getting tired of her asking—she could see it in their faces—and they no doubt wondered how Corrine had managed to feed thousands of soldiers, often under extreme conditions, but couldn't run a small kitchen with a staff of ten.

She wondered the same thing herself.

"Employees aren't soldiers," Jake had gently reminded her more than once. "And what motivates them to do a good job is different than what you're used to. If you want to win them over, you're going to have to modify your techniques."

And therein lay the problem. Corrine might have been honorably discharged after eight years of exemplary service, preceded by four years in the ROTC, but in her heart, she was still a member of the U.S. Army Corps and probably always would be. She'd lived a large part of her life in a world where orders were obeyed without question, and certainly without attitude. Respect was automatically given to anyone of higher rank. Duty and responsibility were placed above all else.

It was a world she liked and missed.

Jake was right when he said employees weren't soldiers. But Corrine didn't think expecting them to do the job and do it well was out of line.

A buzzing timer, signaling that the cherry cobbler was done, snapped her back to the moment. "Luke, go get the vanilla ice cream."

The lanky eighteen-year-old shuffled toward the walk-in freezer.

Gerrie mouthed to Pat, *"She could ask nice,"* then blushed and averted her head when she realized Corrine had been watching.

Luke emerged a moment later toting a twenty-gallon tub of ice cream. He dumped it on the closest counter. "This is only a third full, and it's all we got."

"What do you mean? I ordered a new shipment last week. It was supposed to be here yesterday!"

"Guess it didn't come." Luke shrugged.

"Gerrie." Corrine whirled on her assistant cook. "Didn't you follow up like I told you?"

"Yeah." The other woman's defenses visibly shot up. "They said there was a snag and to expect delivery today."

"Well, it's today. Five in the afternoon to be exact, and there's no ice cream." Corrine pressed both hands to her head. "We have two hundred guests expecting cherry cobbler à la mode, and enough ice cream for maybe fifty of them." Her gaze landed on Gerrie. Hard. "What happened?"

"I…forgot. I'm sorry," she answered in a voice that shook. With chagrin? Embarrassment?

More likely anger, thought Corrine.

"Don't let it happen again," she said with a calm she didn't feel. The slip was inexcusable and deserved a reprimand. She didn't give it, however. She couldn't afford to have another employee walk out. Not today. "How much whipping cream do we have?"

"Enough for the cobbler." Gerrie had regained her composure.

"Snap to it."

A second employee jumped in to help.

Corrine opened the oven, squeezing her eyes shut against a blast of hot air, and put in a dozen loaves of the garlic bread. She chided herself for the tiny twinge of remorse she felt over her treatment of Gerrie. Her assistant cook had failed at her task. Not only had she forgotten to follow up with the late delivery, she hadn't told Corrine about it.

Two strikes. In the army…

Employees aren't soldiers.

Corrine swallowed the painful lump that had formed unexpectedly in the back of her throat. She refused to cry. Not here. Not now. Not in front of the employees. Forget her pride; this dinner was too important.

The Tuckers were welcoming a special guest tonight, someone who would be staying with them for six weeks over the summer: Greg Pfitser, professional fisherman, bestselling author and star of the hit cable TV show *Fishing with Pfitser*.

Bear Creek, which ran through the three hundred acre ranch, offered some of the best trout fishing in Arizona, if not the entire southwestern United States. It was stocked from nearby hatcheries and fed by mountain springs, and record-breaking rainbows and Apaches were pulled from its waters on a regular basis, making the ranch a favorite recreation spot for amateur and professional fishermen alike.

Personally, Corrine wasn't all that impressed with their celebrity guest, but the trout-fishing tournament he was hosting in early August would give the ranch a much-needed boost. Twelve years away hadn't diminished her love for her family, and Corrine would do almost anything for them, including biting her tongue.

"Hey, there's a dog in here!" Luke appeared in the pantry doorway, a fifty pound sack of sugar in his arms.

"A dog?" several people echoed.

"It's in the garbage."

Corrine flew across the kitchen, following the same winding path she'd taken earlier. "How the heck did it get in here?"

"Dimitri must have left the door open."

"Who?"

"The guy who just quit."

"Yeah, right." *Dimitri?* Where had she gotten the name Donny?

Corrine reached the pantry and came to a halt. She stared at the floor, horrified. There *was* a dog in her kitchen. At least, she thought it was a dog. A stubby tail attached to a pair of short black-and-white legs stuck out from a spilled bag of trash. A bag that should not have been left by the back door to be tripped over or ransacked by small scavengers.

"Where'd it come from?" one of the helpers asked.

"I don't know." Because of the danger from wild animals that occasionally wandered into the ranch, or the possibility of being kicked or trampled by one of the horses, guests weren't allowed to have pets in their cabins. "It must be a stray."

"A hungry stray." Luke dumped the sack of sugar on the nearest counter.

"Hey," Corrine said sternly to the dog's backside. "Get out of there."

The stubby tail wagged in response.

"Luke, grab him."

"Seriously?"

"We can't have a dog in the kitchen. The health department will shut us down."

"I ain't grabbing no strange dog. What if it bites me?"

Corrine was about to rephrase her order with more authority when Jake's gently delivered advice came back to her. If the dog did indeed bite Luke, there would be more than a workmen's compensation claim to pay. He could sue the ranch, the Tuckers and Corrine.

Definitely not the army anymore.

"Fine. I'll do it."

She reached down, clasped the dog by its middle and pulled. The animal's toenails scraped across the linoleum floor as she did, raising the hairs on the back of her neck. Fortunately, it didn't seem inclined to bite. How could it with a plastic bread bag halfway down its throat?

"Don't eat that." With one hand on the dog's collar—it definitely wasn't a stray—Corrine ripped the bag from its mouth. "You'll choke and die."

In a flash, the dog twisted around and went for her hand— to lick, not bite. She couldn't resist and gave its head a good scratching. Until she'd left for college, she and her three sisters had always owned a dog or two and a couple of cats.

"That's one ugly dog," Luke said, with more emotion than

Corrine had heard him display in all the time they'd worked together.

She had to agree. Rounded mouse ears sat atop a wide, squished-in face with loose, floppy lips and bulging eyes. The dog opened its mouth to pant, and a huge pink tongue fell out the side.

"I think it's kind of cute," another helper said.

"All right, people, back to work. We have a dinner to serve in fifteen minutes."

The staff returned to their tasks, and Corrine bent to lift the dog, intending to shut it in the employee restroom and then phone maintenance. One problem. It didn't want to go, not when there was more trash to investigate. While she attempted to get a solid hold around its middle, the animal nosed through broken eggshells and an empty half-gallon can of cherry pie filling.

"Don't your owners ever feed you?"

She had its back legs suspended in midair when the door to the kitchen banged opened. Corrine wasn't sure which of them, her or the dog, jumped higher.

"I see her," called a high-pitched voice. "She's in here."

"Hurry," said a second voice.

From the sound of the pounding footsteps, Corrine guessed that young children were about to converge on the kitchen. Great. What else could go wrong today?

She grunted and stood, the squirming, licking dog locked firmly in her grip. With a sense of triumph, she spun, ready to deliver a tirade to the careless juvenile owners about dogs on the ranch. The words died on her lips.

The children, two bright-eyed, grinning cherubs, weren't alone. A man was with them. A very tall man. Corrine had to tip her head back to get a good look at him.

"I see you found Belle," he said with the laziest, sexiest drawl she'd ever heard.

Not since her sophomore year in high school had a member of the opposite sex disarmed Corrine. Handsome faces and broad shoulders didn't impress her. She'd seen plenty of them in the army and knew what was inside a man counted for a whole lot more, especially if lives were in the balance.

She handed the wiggling dog to its young owners. "Belle?" she asked.

"It's French for beautiful." Matching dimples cut into the man's ruggedly chiseled cheeks. A lock of dark, wavy hair refused to lie flat and fell charmingly over twinkling brown eyes.

"Which confuses me. Don't take this wrong, but your dog is ugly."

"Not to everyone."

Corrine's gaze went to the children, who were obviously overjoyed at being reunited with their pet and just as obviously indifferent to its Peter Lorre-like features.

"And, since she's a French bulldog," the man added, "the name fit."

Did he ever stop smiling?

Corrine's shield, the one she'd honed long before joining the army, dropped into place. "I'm sorry to inform you, but guests aren't allowed to have dogs on the ranch. You're going to have to keep it—her—in your cabin until you can make other arrangements."

"I do apologize for the mess she made, but here's the thing," he said smoothly. "The owners gave me permission."

"Really?" Corrine drew back. She didn't remember any such exception to ranch rules being raised at the last family business meeting. "And who was that?"

His smile widened rather than diminished, proving that, unlike most people, whether soldier or civilian, he wasn't the least bit intimidated by her. "Jake Tucker and Millie Sweetwater."

Hmm. Corrine's cousin and mother. She'd have to speak to them and find out what was going on.

"Well, I'm one of the owners, too. And I don't remember giving my permission."

"You are?" He took in her disheveled appearance with the same aggravating laziness. "I'm Greg Pfitser," he said, and extended his hand.

The professional fisherman. Their guest of honor at tonight's dinner. The pieces fell suddenly into place. No wonder her family had bent the rules in order to accommodate him.

To her great annoyance, she'd have to bend them, too. Except where her kitchen was concerned.

"Corrine Sweetwater." She accepted his outstretched hand and liked that he returned her grip with equal strength. Weak handshakes, in her opinion, were a sign of weak character. "Welcome to Bear Creek Ranch."

"Thank you." He released her hand only when she gave a slight tug. "Any relation to Millie?"

Corrine didn't like that she needed a moment to collect herself before answering. "Guilty as charged. I'm her daughter. The ranch is family owned and operated."

"These are my kids, Annie and Benjamin."

"Ben," the boy corrected, while craning his neck to avoid slobbery dog kisses.

Corrine looked down at the children. She remembered someone telling her they were twins and…what? Five years old?

"Permission aside, you are going to have to keep the dog on a leash at all times when outside your cabin, and away from public areas. Which includes the kitchen." When they didn't immediately get the message, she clarified, her tone authoritative, "Take the dog outside now."

When they still didn't respond, their father said calmly, "Go on, now."

The twins all but ignored him, apparently more interested in fighting over which of them got to carry the dog outside.

"Hurry," he reiterated, in a tone only marginally firmer.

Through sheer willpower, Corrine kept her mouth shut. Her family wouldn't be happy if she offended their all-important guest by criticizing his parenting skills. Finally, the children left, each carrying one end of the dog.

"Please excuse me," she said, backing away. "We have a dinner to serve." A quick glance told her her staff was no-where close to being ready. Everyone was too busy gawking at Greg.

Dinner would be late again.

"Will I see you in the dining hall?" His brows lifted inquisitively.

"Yes, you will." Corrine was required to make an appearance at most meals and mingle with the guests—a part of her job she didn't particularly like.

"I look forward to it." He waved to the staff on his way to the back door. His gait, like everything else about him, was unhurried. "Nice meeting all of you."

"Same here," Gerrie called. She wasn't alone in falling over herself to bid him goodbye.

Corrine returned to her station. "Make sure there are plenty of appetizers on the tables." Maybe the guests would grumble less about waiting if they had coconut shrimp and chicken wings to munch on.

Next week, she promised herself, *no late dinners.* Whatever it took, she would get her staff back on track. They might not like her or her management techniques, but they would just have to get used to both.

"Wow," Gerrie exclaimed to her friend Pat. "Was he hot or what?"

"Majorly." Pat poured the rest of the freshly whipped cream into a huge tub. "And so nice. I'm setting my TV remote to the Outdoor Channel the minute I get home. Anyone know what time his show airs?"

For the first time since Corrine took over as kitchen manager, the workers pulled together like a real team. Dinner was late, but only by a few minutes, and went out the door without a hitch. Luke even changed his mind and offered to stay late and help with the dishes.

Corrine should have been glad. Instead, her irritation with Mr. Fishing with Pfitser—and herself—increased. He'd accomplished in a matter of minutes what she'd failed to do in weeks—bring harmony to her kitchen.

Removing her apron and hat, she readied herself for her appearance in the dining hall, intent on avoiding him if possible. Unfortunately, the instant she stepped into the dining room, her cousin Jake hailed her to join him, their special guest and his two children.

She couldn't refuse. Not when her family had so much riding on the success of the fishing tournament and Mr. Pfitser's stay.

UPTIGHT WOMEN FASCINATED Greg. Oh, they were wrong for him, he knew. Boy, did he know it. But there was something about Corrine Sweetwater that was hard to resist.

"This is delicious," he said, taking a bite of lasagna.

"Thank you."

"Jake tells me you recently left the army."

"Yes."

"Ever serve in the Middle East?"

"Twice during the last four years."

"Always in food service?"

"No. Also as a mechanical engineer."

Whatever questions he asked, Corrine kept her answers short and to the point. And her attention, he noticed, continually wandered. Not in a distracted manner. Rather, she checked the waitstaff, the guests, the many rows of picnic-style tables, the level of beverages in the self-serve dispensers, the food coming out the door and the dirty dishes going in.

Uptight *and* a workaholic—which made her that much more fascinating and that much more off-limits.

"What made you enlist, can I ask?"

"I was ROTC in college." It hadn't been Corrine's first choice, but after losing her athletic scholarship to Arizona State University because of something entirely her own fault, she'd taken one of the few remaining options available. In the end, it had worked out for the best, but only because she was lucky.

"What she's not telling you," her mother interjected, "is that she put herself through school. Her father and I are very proud of her." Millie patted the arm of the middle-aged man sitting next to her.

"We're proud of all our girls," he said.

"You have sisters?" Greg asked Corrine.

"Three," her mother answered. "Carolina lives here on the ranch. Rachel in town. Violet's out of state, but she visits often and brings our granddaughter with her."

"I can't wait to meet the rest of the family," Greg stated.

"Dad, can we go now?" Ben asked.

"What about dessert?"

"I don't like cherries." Annie pouted. She'd hardly touched her meal, whereas her brother had demolished his.

"Do you like ice cream?" Greg inquired.

"Yes," she said sulkily.

"Maybe Ms. Sweetwater will give you a dish of ice cream without the cherry cobbler." He flashed his most winning smile.

"Of course." Corrine started to rise from her seat beside her cousin.

"Not yet." Greg wrapped an arm around his daughter. "She has to finish more of her dinner first."

Annie scowled at her plate, apparently deciding which food item would be the easiest to choke down, and finally selected the garlic bread. Greg knew from experience the most she'd do was nibble on a corner, and after insisting on one more bite, he'd let it go. As far as parenting went, he sucked. But he'd only been doing it for less than six months, and intermittently at that.

"We're so glad you agreed to accept our invitation," Millie said. "Speaking as someone who grew up on this ranch, I'm sure you couldn't find a better place to spend the summer. Your children will love it here. There's so much to do. Hiking, mountain biking, horseback riding, boating, ATVs, games and—" she smiled at them "—fishing, of course."

"Sounds great, doesn't it, kids?"

"I don't like to fish," Ben announced.

"They're slimly and gross," his sister concurred.

"Really?" Millie appeared surprised.

"Ben and Annie aren't exactly chips off the old block." Greg attempted to make light of what was, to him, a sore subject. "We're going to work on it this summer. Which is one of the reasons I accepted your invitation."

"And we're glad you did. Aren't we, Corrine?"

"Yes, we are."

Millie obviously had as much luck coaxing enthusiasm from her reluctant offspring as Greg did from his.

"Ben and Annie haven't been able to spend a lot of time with me until recently."

Greg didn't bother to explain that their mother had purposely kept their existence a secret. If not for an unexpected coincidence, he might never have found out he was a father. The moment he did, he'd hired the best attorney he could find, and won shared custody, much to their mom's anger and dismay.

He, Ben and Annie were still getting acquainted. The twins were as unaccustomed to having a dad as he was to having children. Hopefully, the six weeks they spent at the ranch would facilitate the process. His children were the reason Greg had jumped at the opportunity when his agent presented it to him, though the tournament at the end of summer wouldn't hurt his book sales or TV ratings.

Greg often wondered when he'd stopped being a fisherman and started being a businessman.

"What was it like growing up here?" he asked.

"It was great," Corrine exclaimed.

There! He saw it. Real emotion shining in her eyes. She obviously loved the ranch and the people on it.

"Would you like me to arrange a tour tomorrow?" Jake asked Greg. "You can check out our best fishing spots and get the lay of the land."

"That'd be nice."

"Can we ride a horse?" Annie asked, still picking at her garlic bread.

"Sure thing." Jake winked at her.

Annie beamed.

Greg wished that his daughter would look at him like that just once. "Thanks."

"I'll have Gary Forrester, our manager of guest amenities, take you and your children around." Jake turned to his cousin. "Or Corrine could. Isn't it your day off?"

She couldn't have looked more startled if he'd stuck her with a red-hot poker. "Yes…well, no. I'm working tomorrow."

"On your day off?" Greg grinned at her, mostly because it would annoy her, and he liked annoying her.

Her susceptibility to teasing wasn't the only thing about Corrine Sweetwater that appealed to him. Her short brown hair, with its sweetly curling ends, might be military regulation, but Greg found it far sexier than any waist-length locks. Probably because the cut made her hazel eyes appear enormous, even without makeup, and enhanced her flawless complexion. Had she not chosen the military as a career, she could have easily succeeded in television.

"The work's piled up." She stood, and this time no one stopped her. "I had an employee quit today."

"Oh, my. Not another one?" Millie tsked. "How many are you going to go through?"

"As many as it takes to find the right ones," Corrine said tersely. "I'll get that dish of ice cream for your daughter," she told Greg.

He watched her walk across the crowded, noisy dining hall to the kitchen, her gait precise, her shoulders squared. She might have been leading her platoon, if not for the slight and very feminine sway of her hips. Did it occur to her that she had the attention of every male in the room, with the possible exception of her father, her cousin and Ben?

Probably not. Greg doubted Corrine had any idea of her profound effect on men. If she did, she'd realize just how attractive Greg found her.

A shame the feeling wasn't mutual.

Then again, maybe not.

Greg needed to focus on his children during the coming weeks, getting to know them and learning how to be a family. At the moment, their relationship was awkward at best. He also had a tournament to prepare for, and two TV shows to film.

The last thing he needed was to become romantically involved with a woman so completely wrong for him.

Chapter Two

The hinge squeaked in protest as Greg shut the cabin door behind him and Belle. He winced and paused on the stoop, relieved that neither of the kids hollered to him.

They were still asleep and probably would be for several more hours. A love of fishing wasn't the only trait the three of them didn't share. While he was up before the crack of dawn most days, Ben and Annie dragged themselves out of bed only when they had to.

Discovering he was a father had come as quite a shock. Greg could have pretended Ben and Annie didn't exist. It certainly was what their mother, Leah, had wanted, what she'd fought tooth and nail for. But he couldn't bring himself to walk away.

Responsibility had less to do with it than a need to right past wrongs. His dad hadn't been much of a father and Greg had been even less of a son. He wanted more for his children, and an opportunity to make amends.

"Sit, Belle."

For once, the dog listened, and Greg bent down to snap a leash to her collar. He'd gotten the little bulldog from a canine rescue organization. The idea had been his mother's. She thought a pet might help Ben and Annie accept their new father and new living arrangement.

They liked the dog all right. Greg, not so much. He intended to change that.

All of a sudden Belle yipped and, tearing the leash from his hand, darted off after a squirrel. It scampered up a tree trunk, easily winning the race. Not taking defeat well, Belle stood at the base of the tree, barking. Greg descended the porch steps with one leap and collected the dog before she woke up the kids and the neighbors.

He and Belle then followed an uneven stone walkway to the narrow dirt road that fronted this particular row of cabins. On the other side lay Bear Creek, not much more than a stone's throw away. Greg figured he had a few minutes to explore and let Belle do her business before returning to check on the kids.

A tour of the ranch probably wasn't necessary, though he would heartily agree if Corrine consented to be his guide. The layout was easy. All roads and trails eventually led to either the main lodge or dining hall or the riding stables. At least, all the marked roads and trails.

It was those unmarked and less traveled stretches that interested Greg. The more remote the spot, the better the fishing.

Standing on the bank of Bear Creek, he studied the first gray streaks of dawn breaking through the tall pine and oak trees. The size of the creek surprised him, and he guessed there were places up and down the mountainside where it was considerably wider. Deep holes where the fish hid out.

He bent and unsnapped Belle's leash. They were far enough away from guests and buildings that the dog could run loose for a few minutes without getting into trouble. Nose to the ground, she explored the dense underbrush, her stubby tail wagging a mile a minute.

Apparently, the appearance of one person and his out-of-shape dog wasn't enough to silence the many birds, which became increasingly active as the sun grew brighter and warmer. This was Greg's favorite time of day. Tomorrow, he'd have his pole and tackle box with him, a nice secluded bank picked out, and for once would get to fish without a camera operator and director three feet away.

Maybe just this once the kids wouldn't mind getting up early and coming with him.

Yeah, and maybe they'd stop missing their mother and wanting to go home.

Neither possibility was likely to happen anytime soon.

Belle suddenly stopped her exploring and began barking. Up ahead, the bushes rustled and twigs snapped. Greg froze in his tracks, recalling the last time he'd inadvertently surprised a wild animal. Doing so was one of the hazards of being a professional outdoorsman. Mostly, he'd gotten away unscathed. Mostly.

The dog's barking changed to excited whining.

All at once, a creature burst onto the trail in front of them and came to an abrupt halt. She wore camo shorts, a tan muscle shirt and a backward ball cap. A silver medallion with a military emblem hung from a chain around her neck. Her breathing, which had been rapid, stilled when she caught sight of him.

So did his. Despite her masculine attire, she was the loveliest woman he'd seen in a long time.

"Good morning." He smiled.

She didn't, which was unfortunate. If Corrine Sweetwater ever let down her guard, she'd be dazzling. For a moment, he imagined what it would be like to be the lucky guy who succeeded in helping her do so.

"Morning," she answered briskly, looking a little put out at their chance encounter. "Are you settling in?"

"Not quite unpacked, but we're getting there."

"Good. If you need anything, just call Jake's assistant,

Alice. She'll see you're taken care of." Corrine wiped her forehead with the back of her hand.

The gesture was entirely innocent and completely casual, yet Greg was mesmerized. He issued himself another silent warning. Corrine wasn't his type, wasn't for him. He could look and appreciate what he saw. Nothing more.

"Out for a jog?"

"A run," she corrected, and braced her hands on her hips. "What about you?"

He noticed the heart rate monitoring devise attached to her left wrist. She obviously took her exercise seriously. He could relate, as he felt equally serious about his sport. Perhaps they weren't so different, after all.

"I took your cousin's suggestion and am getting the lay of the land. Know of any good fishing spots?"

"Sorry."

"You don't fish?"

"Not since I was nine."

"Too bad." So much for mutual interests.

She looked past him. "Where are Ben and Annie?"

"Still sleeping. They're not exactly morning people."

"Should you leave them alone?"

"I've only been gone a couple minutes and was just about to head back."

"Okay."

He sensed her disapproval and glanced over his shoulder, reassuring himself that he could see the cabin clearly through the trees. "Isn't it safe here?"

"Generally, yes."

"But what?"

"They're pretty young to be left unsupervised."

"I locked the door." Had he made another mistake? Greg didn't want to admit his ignorance to Corrine. Until a few weeks ago, he'd had only daytime outings with Ben and

Annie, and no more than a dozen at that. Everything he knew about raising five-year-olds could fit on a the head of a pin.

"I'm sure they'll be fine."

He began to have doubts and checked the cabin again. It looked quiet and peaceful. Still, he said, "I should get back."

"Your dog's not on a leash." Corrine frowned.

Irresponsible father, irresponsible pet owner. One more strike and he'd be out.

"Sorry." He removed the leash from his back pocket.

Before he could attach it to Belle's collar, the dog shot between Corrine's legs in hot pursuit of another squirrel. This one also won the race. Greg chased after Belle and caught her a good twenty feet up the trail. When he looked back, Corrine was leaving.

"See you at dinner," he called, again enjoying the view.

"It's my day off." She pressed a button on her wrist monitor and set off at a fast walk. "Don't forget to keep your dog on a leash," she warned, before disappearing into a thick stand of trees.

Greg tried not to dwell on his disappointment. Turning around, he went back to the cabin. After Corrine's not-so-subtle reprimand, he half expected to find Ben and Annie missing, abducted by a crazed kidnapper. He could already hear Leah's screech of alarm when he phoned her.

What he discovered when he opened the cabin door wasn't reason enough to call the authorities, but it wasn't good, either.

His sleep-in-till-ten children had risen early. The cabin's small living room resembled a war zone. Every article of clothing they'd packed, every shoe, every toy, every toiletry, was strewn about, hanging off furniture, dropped in corners and dangling from lamp shades. Streams of toilet paper crisscrossed the floors. Sheets of paper—his latest script?—had been crumpled into balls.

Greg grumbled to himself. Corrine had been right; he shouldn't have left Ben and Annie alone.

Belle rushed inside to investigate a toppled over trash can.

"Hey, guys," he said into the empty room. "Where are you?"

Two small faces peaked out from behind the tiny kitchenette counter.

Greg swallowed the anger surging inside him. "Let's get this cleaned up or you won't go horseback riding today."

"You're not going to yell at us?" Ben asked, his expression wary.

"No."

"Really?" He and Annie crept slowly out from behind the counter.

"Really." Greg hadn't lashed out at anyone since he was seventeen, nor would he. Especially his children.

He'd grown up with a father who hadn't known how to speak to his family in a normal tone of voice. His hair-trigger temper had ruined any possibility for a loving and healthy relationship with those around him, and had ultimately ended his life at the much too early age of forty-nine.

All these years later, Greg had yet to forgive himself for being the one to cause his father's death.

CORRINE DIDN'T LIKE using the phone in the kitchen. As a warrant officer, she'd had her own office, small though it was, and grown accustomed to conducting business in private. Since there were no empty offices in the main lodge, she made her calls from Jake's. Alice would buzz Corrine in the kitchen and let her know when Jake was at lunch or out on appointments. While not perfect, the system worked.

She left the kitchen and cut across a narrow patch of grass separating the dining hall from the main lodge. The air, a temperate seventy-four degrees according to the thermometer, felt refreshing after the sweltering kitchen. On the main road, a long string of horses walked, wranglers leading the guests on a trail ride. A rowdy game of shuffleboard was under way in the court next to the pool. The activity was good to see after the decrease of guests in recent months. While reservations were steady, according to Alice's latest report, they were still short of the family's goal. Greg Pfitser's presence and the tournament would, they all hoped, change that.

Corrine sighed as she hurried along. Her so-called day off had thus far consisted of helping with the breakfast cleanup and making yet another switch in the day's menu. Seems no one had bothered with the egg count the last two days. Not only would tuna sandwiches be substituted for egg salad at lunch. Corrine would also need to decide what to substitute for omelets at tomorrow's breakfast.

She mentally ticked off her list of calls to make. First, the ice cream vender, to find out what had happened to their shipment. Next, a rush order for an extra hundred dozen eggs. Last, contacting the nearby community college and posting an ad with student resources for a dishwasher.

The problems she experienced at her family's ranch were nothing like those she'd had in the army. Resolving them wasn't the same, either. She kept telling herself it shouldn't be so hard. But it was and that frustrated her. If only civilian life were more like the service.

If only she could change to fit her new—make that old—surroundings.

When she pushed open the door to the main lobby, a bell overhead tinkled. For as long back as Corrine could remember, a bell heralded the arrival of visitors to the historic guest ranch nestled at the base of the Matazal Mountains.

"Hi, how's it going?" Natalie, their manager of guest services, greeted Corrine from behind the front desk.

"All right."

"Jake's still in his office if that's where you're heading."

"Oh." Corrine paused just inside the long pine counter with its beveled edges and beautifully engraved scrollwork. "Alice called me and said he was leaving."

"That was before one of the maintenance guys reported a broken pipe in cabin eleven. The bathroom's apparently flooded."

"What about the guests?"

"Luckily, the water had only reached the hall before we stopped it. None of their stuff was touched."

"Good." Corrine studied the charmingly appointed lobby with its green checkered curtains, polished hardwood floors and braided area rugs. Most people would relish sitting and relaxing for a few minutes in one of the overstuffed couches. She wasn't most people. "I think I'll head back to the kitchen. Can you give me a holler when he leaves?"

She no sooner spoke than Jake came out of his office, briefcase in hand, cowboy hat on his head. "Hey," he said upon spotting her. "What's up?"

"Just came by to borrow your office. I need to make some calls."

"Isn't this your day off?"

"It was." She rounded the counter and headed toward him. "But like you, I can't seem to break away."

"Don't tell me you didn't get any days off in the army." He held his office door open and waited for her to enter ahead of him.

"Of course I did. But I also had competent and dependable help to cover for me." Too late, she realized her slip. A backward glance over her shoulder confirmed that Natalie had heard the unkind remark. Corrine groaned inwardly.

She and Natalie were friends, or had been. Natalie's parents were hired by Corrine's grandfather over thirty years ago. She and Natalie had grown up on the ranch together and were classmates all through school until Corrine left for college. When Natalie's mother retired a few years ago, about the same time Corrine began her second tour in the Middle East, Natalie took over the position as manager of guest amenities.

Last year, she had met and fallen in love with Aaron Reyes when he came to the ranch. The former National Rodeo champion was left widowed when his wife, Jake's sister, had died accidentally. Aaron had recently adopted Natalie's young daughter from a previous relationship.

Like many employees, Natalie's loyalty to the Tuckers ran deep, and not just because of her job. But despite her outward friendliness, Corrine had noticed a change in their former relationship. Disparaging remarks probably didn't help.

Work, she thought glumly, wasn't the only place she needed to modify her techniques. Her social skills were pretty rusty, too.

"You want some coffee?" Jake asked.

"Thanks, but I already had a cup."

He motioned to the couch along the far wall.

"What about the broken pipe?"

"It's handled. I delegated. You should, too."

Corrine pulled her legs under her and wedged her back in the corner cushion, not liking the vulnerable feeling coming over her. Maintaining control was easy around anyone except family. They brought out the worst and—she couldn't deny it—the best in her.

"What's wrong now?" Jake asked, not unsympathetically, as he settled in his chair.

"It's Gerrie."

"She's a good assistant cook."

"In your opinion."

"She's been with us a long time. She knows her job. Don't take this as criticism, but maybe you should start trusting her to do it instead of always peering over her shoulder."

How was Corrine supposed to take what he said other than as criticism?

"I'd stop peering so much if she was on the ball. Two-thirds of the calls I'm making this morning are to fix her screwups."

Jake leaned back, clasped his hands behind his head and rested his boots on the coffee table. "The kitchen is yours to run, and I'm not going to tell you how to do it. But as operations manager, I am going to make periodic suggestions that I hope you'll consider."

This was the strictest approach he'd taken with her since her return, and it showed Corrine just how poorly she was doing.

Her shoulders involuntarily slumped. It shouldn't be this way. She was competent and capable, and had a list of commendations three pages long. She oftentimes set the bar others aspired to reach, one of her superiors had commented during a performance evaluation.

Fat lot of good all those kudos did her now.

"Gerrie has a problem with follow-up," Corrine stated, coming to her own defense. "And with authority. All the employees do."

"No, they just have a problem with your style of authority."

"Olivia was tough," Corrine said, referring to her predecessor and one-time role model.

After more than two decades as kitchen manager, Olivia Hernandez had retired. Her announcement came about the same time Corrine was considering not reenlisting, and felt a little like destiny.

"Olivia *was* tough," Jake concurred. "But only when people weren't doing their jobs."

"Well, I have people not doing their jobs."

"You have a staff adapting to change. A rocky transition is sometimes part of the process." He cleared his throat. "Losing dishwashers right and left isn't helping. It's not good for morale and not good for you. You need a day off now and then."

Corrine frowned. Of all the adjustments to civilian life she'd anticipated, difficulty performing her job wasn't one of them.

"I don't want Gerrie to quit," Jake said. "You hear me? You need to make this work."

For a second, he'd sounded so much like her former commanding officer that Corrine was tempted to answer, "Yes, sir."

"Fine."

"And I don't want you to quit, either," he added. "You're not just the new kitchen manager, you're family."

If he thought she was about to let a minor personnel problem run her off the ranch, then he really didn't know her well. He certainly didn't realize the level of her commitment and determination. Corrine hadn't risen in rank because she was afraid to meet challenges. She'd risen in rank because she met and overcame them.

She would meet and overcome this challenge, too.

"Promise me when you're done with your phone calls, you'll take a break from the kitchen."

She shrugged in reply.

"I want you to give Greg Pfitser and his children a tour of the ranch."

Corrine sat bolt upright. "I thought Natalie was going to do that."

"She was. But when I contacted Greg, he asked if we could

reschedule for after lunch. Something apparently came up with the kids. He wasn't specific."

It was on the tip of Corrine's tongue to ask why Natalie couldn't also reschedule, but she refrained.

Jake evidently picked up on her unspoken question, for he said, "We have a number of check-ins arriving this afternoon and no one to cover the front desk."

Corrine silently fumed. She really didn't want to give Greg Pfitser and his children a tour of the ranch, and considered making up something about a previous commitment. But she knew Jake would see through her ruse.

She hadn't had a "commitment" outside work since returning to the ranch. Hadn't looked up old school pals and gotten together. Hadn't rented her own place in town. Hadn't even purchased a car. And she certainly hadn't dated.

No wonder Greg Pfitser made her uncomfortable. Her social skills weren't so rusty that she didn't recognize attraction when it followed her across a crowded dining room or up a wooded trail, as his eyes did. She tried to remember the last time a man had stared at her with undisguised interest.

Hector.

The answer came to her immediately, but she pushed it out of her mind. Memories of him were too painful to dwell on.

"He may not need a tour of the ranch," she said referring to Greg. "I ran into him this morning during my run, and he seemed to be finding his way around with no problem."

"I want him and his kids to feel welcomed." Jake sat up, plopping his boots on the floor.

"He was walking his dog without a leash."

"You say that like he was caught breaking into a guest's cabin."

"The dog got into the kitchen yesterday."

"I heard. He told us about it at dinner last night and apologized."

Her cousin's nonchalance bothered Corrine. "Do you know what'll happen if someone reports us to the health department? The dog needs to be kept on a leash."

"You're making a mountain out of a molehill."

"And you're making light of my concerns, which I think are valid." Corrine pushed herself to her feet, irritation vanquishing her earlier feeling of vulnerability. "The kitchen, this entire ranch, is important to me. I appreciate everything Greg Pfitser can do for us, the increased business his TV show and the fishing tournament will bring. But we can't give him the run of the place, allow him to break rules that were established for the safety and well-being of our guests, just because he's a minor celebrity."

"Wow." Jake gawked at her.

Corrine realized with a touch of embarrassment that she'd come close to having an outburst. She lowered her gaze. "Sorry, I didn't mean to rant."

"I like that you're loyal to the family and looking out for us." He also stood and adjusted his hat. "It makes insisting you take the Pfitsers on that tour easier."

"Jake." She wouldn't refuse him. It wasn't in her nature to disobey. But for once, she wished someone would understand her reservations without her having to explain.

"Do it for the family." He hooked an arm around her neck and tugged her against his chest, much as he'd done when she was a kid and he the older, wiser, annoying-big-brother-ish cousin. "Please."

"You're choking me," she complained.

"Come on," Jake cajoled. "You're the only family member free today. And besides, it'll do you some good to get out with people besides us."

"Okay." Corrine relented, not because she'd changed her mind but because it was her duty.

And duty was something she related to, something she used to hold the pieces of her life together when it was falling apart, like it had eighteen months ago.

Everyone thought her decision not to re-up, not to put in her twenty, was so she could return home to Arizona and help with the family business, filling a vital position left void by the departing kitchen manager. It was the reason she gave and one that people didn't question.

It was also a bald-faced lie.

Chapter Three

Corrine halted in midstep at the sound of something heavy hitting the water.

Ben stood by the edge of the pool, his expression a mixture of guilt and defiance. Annie, his ever present shadow, huddled behind him.

Corrine waited for Greg to scold his children. It didn't happen. Ben tossed another rock into the pool. She bit her tongue.

"Don't do that, Ben," Greg said. The warning, too little too late, in Corrine's opinion, was delivered as casually as a comment on the weather. "Is the pool heated?" He peered into the turquoise-blue water, at the bottom of which now sat two large rocks.

Where had Ben got them? He must have taken them from one of the planters near the chaise longues.

"Not during the summer," she answered, still distracted. Should she get the pool skimmer and make Ben retrieve the rock, or let Maintenance do it? "The Jacuzzi is, however." It was then she heard the unmistakable *ping, ping, ping* of a stick being banged on the wrought-iron fence.

Ben and Annie were at it again.

Corrine had reached her limit. So far, the children had touched everything, gone everywhere and done everything they were told not to. Badminton birdies had wound up in the gutter, horseshoes were lost in the bushes and muddy footprints covered the lobby floor. Now, rocks were in the pool and, possibly, chips in the recently painted fence. And they were only ninety minutes into the tour of the ranch.

Through all the children's misbehaving, Greg had done nothing. Okay, not nothing, but Corrine didn't count a quiet, "Come on, you two," as taking action. She thought of the horseback ride coming up later and shuddered. Those poor horses. Those poor guests!

She, thank goodness, wouldn't be there to see. Once she dropped the Pfitsers off at the stables, she'd be done with them. Hopefully, for good. Maybe the wranglers could get the children to behave. Their father certainly couldn't. Or wouldn't.

"Do you ever use the Jacuzzi?"

Greg's question had Corrine shaking her head to clear it. "No."

"That's a shame."

She tensed, not sure how to interpret his remark. Was he flirting with her or simply making casual conversation?

"What would you like to see next?"

He straightened to his full height. At five-eight, Corrine was no shorty. Greg had a good six inches on her and gave her the rare sensation of being petite.

"What do you suggest?"

She tried to think of an activity that would entertain the Pfitser children while keeping them out of trouble. "Do the kids like riding bikes?"

"I...don't know."

That, thought Corrine, was a strange answer. Weren't parents supposed to know those things about their children? She observed Ben and Annie, who'd taken the cover off the leaf trap and were sticking their hands inside.

"We could ask them," she prompted.

"Okay."

Greg's obvious hesitancy mystified her. Something was definitely a bit off with the Pfitsers.

Finally, he said, "Ben, Annie. Do you know how to ride bikes?"

They glanced up from what they were doing, leaves and pine needles clutched in their fists. Corrine couldn't wait to see what Ben did with his prize or where he threw it.

"No," he said.

Annie concurred by adding, "We're not allowed to."

"Not allowed?" Corrine spoke sharply and, she immediately realized, without thinking.

"They live with their mother in downtown Denver," Greg said. "There aren't any places to ride a bike."

"Oh." His explanation made sense, she supposed. Only why hadn't he known that to begin with? "I guess we could take the golf cart."

"Where to?"

Greg flashed her a smile that would have sent a rush of tingles skittering up a weaker woman's spine. In Corrine's case, there was only one tingle. But undeniably a tingle, much to her annoyance. She didn't like finding Greg attractive, and liked his response to her even less.

"Around the rest of the ranch. Or there are some ruins not too far away."

"Indian ruins?"

"An old burial ground, according to local legend. Two bodies were found there years ago and moved to the town cemetery."

Greg grimaced, and Corrine couldn't resist laughing. The man cleaned fish for a living. She wouldn't have pegged him as having such a low "eww" factor.

In the span of a single heartbeat, his smile changed from

sexy to positively lethal. It sent another of those annoying tingles dancing up her spine.

"That's nice," he said, and moved toward her slowly. Very slowly.

"What's nice?" Dang, but he was tall. She willed herself not to back up a step.

"You laughed. I was pretty sure you had it in you, but then—"

Whatever he'd intended to say was cut short by a high-pitched scream, followed by a loud splash.

Annie had fallen in the pool.

Greg started running.

So did Corrine. "Can she swim?"

"I don't know."

Corrine didn't have time to absorb his remark and wonder, yet again, why he didn't know basic information about his own children.

Annie's head broke the surface of the water near the edge of the pool. Good thing. Greg had looked ready to jump in and save her. He knelt and reached an arm down, easily hauling her out of the water and setting her on the deck.

The instant she caught her breath, she started crying.

"It's okay." Greg awkwardly patted her back. "You're fine now."

"I'll get a towel." Corrine hurried through the pool gate and around the corner to the sauna. Removing a ring of keys from her belt loop, she opened a locked storage cupboard. The towels were thin and scratchy, but Annie probably wouldn't care.

Corrine returned quickly to the scene of the crime and held out the towels to Greg. He'd carried his daughter to one of the nearby patio chairs and sat with her on his lap. Ben stood off to the side, shifting uneasily. An unpleasant suspicion began to form on the fringes of Corrine's mind.

"Thanks," Greg said. He wrapped a towel around Annie' shoulders and placed another across her legs. "What hap pened, honey?"

She pointed a shaky finger at her brother and sobbed. "H pushed me."

Greg stared at his son, shock registering on his face. "Di you push your sister in the pool?"

"No."

"Liar!" Annie glared at him.

"Ben. Tell the truth." Greg's voice, though firm, remaine calm and casual.

Corrine was astounded. If Ben were her son, she'd b giving him one very big piece of her mind.

"She put leaves in my hair." He brushed a hand over th top of his head. Bits of debris fell like rain onto his shirt.

"That's no reason to push her. She could have been ser ously hurt."

Ben pouted.

"Now, tell your sister you're sorry."

Annie tugged on the ends of the towel, her expressio smug.

Corrine stepped aside, giving Greg privacy to disciplin his errant progeny.

"Ben." He raised his brows expectantly.

"I'm not sorry." The child stuck out his lower lip.

"I think you are."

Corrine didn't envy Greg, having dealt with her share (disciplinary problems in the service. Being firm, standin strong, especially when it involved the safety of others, wa imperative. It hadn't always been easy for her, and she'd mad plenty of mistakes.

One of them costly.

"Okay, Ben." Greg set Annie on her feet and adjusted h

towel. "If you don't apologize, then I guess we don't have to go horseback riding."

The boy remained stubborn.

"Okay. Have it your way."

"What about me?" Annie demanded. "Don't I get to go riding?"

"Well, you put leaves in his hair. That wasn't right, either."

"Not fair." Her face crumpled. Corrine worried she might start crying again.

"We'll talk about this later. Come on, son." Greg motioned to Ben, then said to Corrine, "Can you take us back in the golf cart?"

She left them and walked the short distance to the main lodge, grinding her teeth the entire way and reminding herself she wasn't a parent, children weren't soldiers and she shouldn't be critical of Greg. But gut instinct told her that while his intentions were good, he hadn't handled the situation well.

After borrowing the keys from Natalie, Corrine drove the golf cart to the pool. Greg loaded the children into the rear seat. They were sullen and quiet all the way to the Pfitser cabin. So was Corrine.

She came to a stop in front of the unit. "If you change your mind, there's a trail ride leaving at three o'clock."

Greg helped the children out. "I thought we were going to the ruins."

"We can." Corrine had foolishly hoped to be done with her tour guide duties.

"Daddy, can I unlock the door?" Annie jumped up and down in place. "Please, please."

He reached into his pocket and removed the cabin key. "Here."

The two kids raced up the path, laughing and shouting as

if the last thirty minutes had never happened. Greg didn't follow them.

"What's wrong?" He propped a foot on the running board of the golf cart.

"Nothing."

"Come on." His mouth curved into that much too potent grin of his.

"Really." She stiffened her spine. *No tingle. Not now.*

"Are you upset about what happened at the pool?"

Shut up, Corrine. Don't say a word. He's our special guest and will bring a lot of business to the ranch.

"Of course not."

"Okay." He removed his foot. "We'll only be a few minutes." He started to walk away.

"It's just that pushing someone in the pool is dangerous."

He stopped and turned. "I know."

"And against the rules."

"Okay." His grin faded.

It was like some evil demon had invaded her and taken over her brain, forcing her lips to form the words. No, not a demon. A warrant officer. The one used to people behaving responsibly and putting safety first.

"What if we hadn't been right there? Annie could have drowned."

"But we were right there."

"Ben broke the rules. He should be…" Corrine caught herself an instant before crossing the line.

"Punished?" Greg finished for her. "He is. We're not going horseback riding."

But they were going to the ruins. "That's not what I was going to say."

He didn't look as if he believed her. In fact, he looked perturbed.

"I can talk to Ben if you'd like," she offered. "He might listen better to a stranger."

"I don't like," Greg said tersely. "And I don't like you butting into my personal business."

"It's your personal business as long as it doesn't affect this ranch."

"At which point it becomes yours?"

"I am one of the owners." Her voice rose dangerously high.

His remained level. "My son isn't a danger to your guests. He and his sister quarrel, just like most siblings."

A vision of Jake's angry face filled Corrine's mind. She conceded that she might have overreacted, and tried for a more conciliatory approach with Greg. "I'm only looking out for everyone's well-being, including yours and your children's."

"Funny, I thought for a second you were trying to tell me how to be a good parent."

As much as Corrine disagreed with Greg's soft-handed approach when it came to dealing with Ben and Annie, she would do what was best for her family, and making nice with him fell smack-dab in the middle of that category. Luckily, he would be gone in six weeks.

"Please…excuse me." The words stuck in her throat before she finally choked them out. "I'm used to contending with soldiers. Most of them male. I have a tendency to shout."

"Well, I refuse to shout. I don't believe it accomplishes anything."

The revelation didn't surprise her.

"I particularly don't shout at my kids." He stepped away from the golf cart. "And I expect you, and everyone else here, to respect my wishes and do the same."

With that, he ambled away.

Corrine sat with her hand on the steering wheel. Civilian

life, she mused, would be so much easier if it mimicked the Army. Then, she wouldn't be in a constant quandary about what to do or say.

HORSEBACK RIDING. Why hadn't Greg thought of it before?

He'd relented after Ben apologized to Annie, and for over an hour at the stables, his kids had been enthralled, occupied and, most importantly, behaving. Despite having no experience, they'd immediately gotten the hang of guiding their mounts along the rugged mountain trail, which was more than Greg could say for himself. His horse walked when it should have stood still, trotted when it should have walked, and went left when it should have gone right.

"Daddy, I'm hungry." Annie twisted sideways in the saddle to peer back at him.

How did she do that without falling off?

"You'll have to wait until dinner," he said, trying to untangle the reins from between his fingers. His horse cranked its large head around to give him the eye. "Yeah, yeah, I suck at this," he grumbled under his breath.

"I can't wait until then," Annie complained.

"Okay. Maybe they have a vending machine at the stables." His finicky daughter wanted to eat? Amazing. What other miracles could this horseback riding produce?

He considered asking the wranglers if there were any day-long rides available, and then realized he'd probably be required to go, too. So much for sneaking in some uninterrupted fishing time. And besides, his butt couldn't take another ride. Any longer in the saddle and he'd be standing for a solid week.

Greg wasn't so inexperienced that he hadn't realized young children required adult supervision, and that he couldn't always provide it. He just hadn't anticipated how difficult it would be to hire a nanny, one willing to drive to the ranch and start at five in the morning. The agency he'd contacted before coming had failed to live up to their guarantee. He'd be more than willing to try elsewhere, if there was an elsewhere to try. Payson, the closest town, was small and didn't have a lot of resources.

Corrine had mentioned contacting Jake's assistant, Alice. Maybe he should. Being aggravated with Corrine was no reason to ignore good advice.

"Daddy, we're here."

"I see." Greg almost cried with relief.

Their horses, along with everyone else's, meandered into the open area in front of the barn and made straight for the hitching post. No one needed to tell them the ride was over. Twenty or so guests had gone on this particular trail ride, including a few children around Ben's and Annie's age. Once again, the wheels in Greg's mind began to spin. If he could round up some playmates for his kids...

He'd no sooner dismounted—an impossible feat without the help of a wrangler—when his cell phone rang. It worked only intermittently around the ranch, and he'd almost forgotten he'd brought it with him. Digging the phone out from his shirt pocket, he checked the caller ID before putting it to his ear.

"Hello."

"It's four-fifteen. Where have you been?"

There was no mistaking the chalk-on-a-blackboard voice. "I'm fine, Irene. And how are you?"

"Annoyed. I've been calling you for hours."

"We were on a trail ride, if you can believe it." Greg hobbled over to the corral fence. Sometime during the ride the bones in his legs had turned to sawdust.

"Why aren't you fishing?" She sounded in a panic, as usual.

"That's a good question, for which I have a good answer."

He and his agent were polar opposites. She was intense, energized and a workaholic, whereas Greg was low-key, laid-back and, as the bio on his book cover stated, recreated for a living. The partnership shouldn't have worked, but it did. Wonderfully. Irene carefully and intelligently guided his career, which had skyrocketed the last few years. He, in turn, had put her agency on the map.

"Yoo-hoo! Greg?" Irene said.

"Sorry. I was watching Ben and Annie."

Her voice softened. "How's that going?"

"Not as easy as I would like."

"Give it time, hon. And don't push. They'll come around eventually."

"What about me?"

"We aren't born being good parents. We learn. You will, too."

Greg wasn't so sure. He'd had such a lousy example in his father. His mother had tried her best, but being married to a tyrant had left her with very little emotion and stamina for Greg. He understood that now. As a child, he'd resented her almost as much as he had his father.

"Your crew is arriving tomorrow afternoon." Irene's reminder brought Greg back to the present. "Tell me you're ready for them."

"Not exactly."

"What's the holdup?"

"Two five-year-olds." His attention returned to Ben and Annie. The bones in their legs were functioning just fine, and they ran around in front of the barn, playing a game of tag.

Was it an age thing?

Impossible. He was only thirty-three. Hardly over the hill.

"I understand getting to know and connecting with your

children is important. But we do have a contract. And besides all that lovely money, there's a schedule to keep."

"I know, I know. I'll call you tomorrow." He disconnected after saying good-bye and went in search of Ben and Annie. They were reluctant to leave, and his legs weren't steady enough to give a decent chase. Before his patience ran out, he stopped and waited in the middle of the open area, counting to ten. Then fifty.

Jake Tucker came out of the barn. Corrine was with him, along with a trio of young girls, one of whom Greg thought he'd met the previous night at dinner.

"How was your ride?" Jake asked.

"Great. The kids had a blast."

"What about you?"

"I admit I'm better sitting on a riverbank than in a saddle."

Jake laughed, then said, "You remember my oldest daughter, Briana."

"I do. Nice to see you again."

"And these are my other daughters, Kayla and LeAnne. Their baby sister's at home."

"You have four girls, too?" Corinne was one of four sisters.

"It runs in the family." Jake chuckled good-naturedly. "Briana was just elected captain of her high school equestrian drill team. She and her sisters were setting up for practice tomorrow."

"Congratulations."

Smiling at the girls, Greg sneaked a sideways glance at Corrine, who he'd turned his back on just a couple hours ago. "Thanks for the tour earlier."

"Can I drive you back to your cabin?" Her offer, while polite, wasn't exactly from the heart.

"Thanks, but what I really need to do is scout the creek

for fishing spots." He glanced at his watch and noted he had about two hours of daylight left. "My crew's arriving tomorrow afternoon, and we start shooting the day after. But I'm not sure my legs are up to a hike."

"Corrine will take you in the cart." Jake inclined his head at his cousin.

"I'd be happy to," she said, her jaw hardly moving.

If that was happy, he hated to think what miserable looked like.

"You know—" Greg began, then stopped. "I'll take a rain check if you don't mind. The kids aren't crazy about fishing, and I can't leave them alone."

"Maybe Briana will babysit for you." Jake nudged his daughter forward with the subtlety of a bull elephant. "She has a lot of experience."

"Really?" Greg suddenly saw a bright light shining at the end of the tunnel. "Would you?" he asked the teenager. "If it's not an imposition. I'll pay, of course."

"Sure. I'll take them to dinner and then hang out with them in the game room until you get back."

Greg would have dropped to his knees in gratitude had he been able to rise again without a hand up.

After informing the kids of the change in plans, he sped off with Corrine in the golf cart.

"Do you know where we're going?" he asked about ten minutes into the trip, every one of them spent in silence.

"More or less. The fishing's better on the south leg of the creek." Each bend they rounded took them farther away from the ranch and deeper into the woods.

"I thought you didn't fish." They talked loudly in order to be heard above the golf cart's noisy engine.

"I asked Jake."

"Before or after he volunteered you to be my driver?"

"Does it make a difference?" Her eyes remained glued to the narrow dirt road.

"Yes, it does." Greg waited for her to look at him. "One's an obligation. The other's a favor."

She might be blushing, but he couldn't be sure.

"Is this the place?" he asked when she pulled the golf cart over to the side of the road. In the near distance, water could be heard cascading over rocks.

"According to Jake."

She didn't offer to come with him, and he didn't request her company.

"If I'm not back in half an hour, come looking for me." He crawled out of the golf cart, wincing when his feet made contact with solid ground. "I hope the bank's not too steep."

At the touch of Corrine's fingers on his arm, he went instantly still. The first time had been nice. This time, the sensation was electric.

"I'm sorry," she said. "I overreacted at the pool."

He had the feeling she didn't apologize often. "Me, too. So I guess we're even."

She removed her hand and returned it to the steering wheel. "Not exactly. You and your children are our guests."

While he was no longer sure she should assume the larger share of the blame, he wasn't against using her guilt to his advantage. Especially if there was even a remote chance of some more mutual touching.

"You can make it up to me if you want."

"How's that?" she asked cautiously.

He grinned, the pain in his legs completely forgotten. "Come fishing with me in the morning."

Chapter Four

Corrine was missing work again. In order to go fishing, of all things. She'd also missed her morning stretch and run. Not that her muscles would suddenly seize up from one skipped workout session, but she liked routine. It helped her stay focused and cope—with the day-to-day ups and downs as well as the big stuff. Like the death of someone she cared for.

Thinking of Hector always reopened old wounds, and she was in no shape to handle another emotional bleeding. Not today. Instead, she concentrated on the man in front of her.

Greg Pfitser.

He stood in the middle of the creek, in water up to his knees, a fishing pole in his hand, a ridiculous hat on his head and an expression of pure contentment on his face. Nothing broke his concentration. Not the water that had splashed on him, soaking his pants above the rubber boots he wore, or the honeybees buzzing past their heads in search of wildflowers.

Corrine understood the enjoyment Greg derived from his job and his commitment to it, even if she didn't like fishing. For six and a half years, she'd felt similarly about the army. Then Hector had died, and almost overnight military service stopped being her calling. Only one thing had kept her going those last ten months: the thought of getting out and going home.

A loud splashing from Greg's direction dragged her from the past to the present. It took her a moment to realize what had happened.

"Did you catch a fish?"

"Hooked one," he said, lifting the pole and cranking the reel. "Catching it is an entirely different matter." The more line he reeled in, the more the pole bent, pulled by the fish beneath the water.

"Don't let it get away."

Corrine watched him from her nearby perch on the bank, admittedly a little enthralled. He was surprisingly graceful for a man his size, and doing something she'd considered silly, if not a colossal waste of time. His movements were those of an athlete or a dancer, elegant and powerful and very precise. Corrine had never seen anything like it and could have sat watching him for hours.

With a final jerk and a lot of splashing, Greg pulled a nice size trout from the creek. Tucking his pole close to this chest, he captured the fish with his free hand and turned it around, apparently inspecting it.

Without thinking, Corrine clapped and blurted, "Good job."

Greg smiled at her. Instantly, the excitement coursing through her took on an entirely different and highly sensual nature. She froze, shocked and more than a little mortified at her reaction. Luckily, Greg didn't notice. The flopping fish garnered his full attention. He grasped it more firmly, then quickly and deftly removed the hook.

Corrine turned away in an effort to compose herself. What the heck had just happened? It was as if she'd become some-one else. She had no interest in fishing, didn't clap when someone caught a fish and certainly didn't get all hot and bothered by a mere smile, even if the guy doing the smiling was drop-dead gorgeous.

Greg bent and released the trout into the shimmering water of the creek.

"Aren't you going to keep it and eat it?" she asked, hoping to defuse the sexual undercurrents—one-way undercurrents, from what she could see—with small talk.

"Would you have cooked it for me if I did?"

"Sure."

"Really?" After pulling a small jar from his vest pocket and rebaiting his hook with a glob of some sort of icky stuff, he cast his line again. "Dinner at Corrine's place. I'm intrigued."

So much for defusing sexual undercurrents. "I meant I'd fix the fish for you at the dining hall," she said, when she'd managed to uncurl her toes.

He chuckled, and she realized he'd been teasing her.

"That wasn't funny," she said, bristling more from chagrin than anger.

"For an ex-soldier, you're pretty gullible."

"For a nice guy, you're pretty mean."

He used his free hand to push his hat back on his head. She noticed his killer dimples were out in full force. "You think I'm nice?"

"Yes."

What she didn't say—but wanted to, oh, so badly—was that she thought he was *too* nice and *too* easygoing. He and Corrine couldn't be more different, and his attitude drove her crazy. Why, then, did she find him…likable? And appealing?

Clearly, she was having a bigger problem adjusting to civilian life than she'd first thought.

Granted, she'd only been in two serious relationships, one in high school and the other in the army. Even so, she was no stranger to the male species. She'd worked with thousands of them. And lack of confidence around them, turning beet-red at the least little teasing, was never one of her problems.

For reasons beyond her comprehension, Greg elicited the most annoying feminine responses in her. It was frustrating and something she needed to nip in the bud right away, before she did something silly like...flirt.

He began walking down the creek with the current. "Coming?" he called over his shoulder.

"I really need to get to work."

She dreaded to think what disasters were awaiting her after being gone from the kitchen since yesterday afternoon, or how many complaints had been lodged at the front desk. On a positive note, the egg vendor had made a special emergency delivery last evening. Gerrie should be able to handle the breakfast service until Corrine arrived.

"I'll help with the dishes," Greg said, flashing her a better-hurry-up look. "Briana's watching the kids until lunch."

Corrine stood grudgingly and dusted off her shorts. If she continued stalling, he'd disappear from sight.

"How much longer are you going to be? This is the third spot you've fished since we started."

"Thirty minutes, I promise," he answered, navigating the rocky creek bottom and rushing water. Though it must have been hard, he made it appear easy.

Corrine couldn't say the same for herself on the overgrown bank. Branches and vines clawed at her face, tree roots reached up to catch the toes of her hiking boots and holes appeared out of nowhere, throwing her off balance.

"Are you okay?"

"I'm fine," she grumbled, dodging a patch of poison ivy. "Maybe I should go back and get the golf cart. That way we won't have so far to walk when you're done."

"We're only going around this next bend." He moved his pole from side to side as he walked, his focus on the bouncing bobber. "I want to test at which depth the fish are more active."

She shouldn't have agreed to come fishing with him, shouldn't have felt guilty about her angry flare-up yesterday, shouldn't have let him convince her to leave the golf cart. At the bottom of the hill, she squirmed through a particularly thick cluster of brush and came out on the other side. The sight greeting her caused her breath to leave her lungs with a soft, "Ooh."

Pole in hand, Greg stood in the middle of a quiet pool, wearing that very contented, very endearing expression again. Sunlight glinted off the water's surface like a million liquid diamonds. A pair of deer, initially startled into immobility, abruptly sprinted off and were swallowed by the woods.

Corrine started breathing again.

Greg really was a joy to watch, and for a few seconds, she was almost glad she'd missed work.

"This is a beautiful spot," she mused out loud.

He glanced up. "You've never been here?"

"No. Not that I remember. I've been gone a long time, too."

"I thought you grew up on the ranch."

"Technically, we lived in Payson," she answered. "But I was here almost every day and stayed overnight a lot."

She found a relatively flat boulder on which to sit. By the time she settled, Greg had caught another fish. Like the first one, he released it back into the water after removing the hook.

"I think I'll bring the film crew here tomorrow."

She'd heard something about them taping segments for his cable TV show during his stay. "What about Ben and Annie?"

"They don't like to fish."

She remembered hearing that, too. "Maybe you could change their minds. They are your kids and must have been born with the same fishing gene." She propped her elbows on her knees and absently played with her medallion. "My father was only a weekend fisherman, but he dragged me and my sisters with him when he could convince us to go."

"Actually, they've never come fishing with me." Greg cast his freshly baited line into the tranquil pool. At the other end, small winged insects fluttered down to the surface one by one to sip at the water. "I've never taken them anywhere except the park, a movie once, and out for fast food."

"Really? Then how do you know they don't like to fish?"

"Their mother told me."

Corrine sensed some discord in Greg's tone and probably should have dropped the subject. Only she didn't. "Traveling so much must make it really hard to be an involved parent."

"My schedule's not the problem." His customary grin flatlined. "I met Ben and Annie for the first time three months ago. Before then, I had no idea I was a father."

Corrine had to stop herself from falling off the boulder.

GREG COULD COUNT on four fingers the number of individuals he'd told about Ben and Annie. They were either family or close friends, not people he'd met a mere two days earlier.

Corrine said nothing, even after regaining her balance. Instead, she waited for him to elaborate. The prospect of spilling his guts to her wasn't half as scary as he'd thought it would be, which surprised him.

"Leah, their mother, and I met when I went home to Wyoming. My mom had to have back surgery, so I took a break to care for her. The forced confinement was difficult for both of us. Her, because she was bedridden, and me because I wasn't used to staying in one place more than a week. Plus I'm not much of a nurse. Or a housekeeper."

The fish had apparently abandoned the pool to swim down the creek. Greg took advantage of the lull to wade closer to

the bank and closer to Corrine. She had yet to comment o
his story. He'd either struck her dumb or she sensed his nee
to talk without interruptions.

It figured that the one gal completely wrong for him woul
be a good listener.

"Leah lived on the same street as my mother. How cliché i
that? The girl next door. She was a mortgage broker—still is
for that matter. Nine years older than me, divorced and ver
type A career orientated. Not my usual pick for a girlfrienc
but then circumstances weren't exactly normal.

"The relationship was doomed from the start and ende
about the same time my mom recovered. I left and went bac
to work. That Christmas, I visited Mom again. She mentione
Leah had moved to Denver. Neither of us brought up her nam
again for the next five years."

"She was pregnant when she moved away?" Corrin
asked.

Greg swung his pole to the side and reeled in his line
Securing the hook to the lowest ring, he laid the pole on th
ground next to his tackle box. Corrine scooted over, issuin
a silent invitation for him to sit beside her. The boulder wa
large enough for two, barely. Their thighs touched. Concen
trating on his story became suddenly more difficult. For
former soldier wearing camo shorts, hiking boots and a
olive-green T-shirt, she sure smelled nice.

"Yeah, pregnant with twins. And instead of coming afte
me for child support, she did everything in her power to pre
vent me from finding out about the babies, including movin
to another state."

"Can I ask why?"

"The only reason Leah ever gave me was that she didn
want a man in her life. Been there, done that, according to he
And if she did want one, I'm sure he wouldn't be a goof-o
like me."

"You're laid-back but hardly a goof-off."

Greg chuckled. "In those days I was. At least in the eyes of a work fiend like Leah. Fishing is playing, not a real job." He sobered. "She's not the only one who thinks that."

"Are you including me in that group?"

"Should I?" He didn't give her a chance to respond. "I put in forty to sixty hours a week. The only difference is I love what I do, and it's fun. Everyone should be as lucky as me."

"You're right. On both counts. Some people see you as a slacker, and I was one of them."

"Was? As in you've changed your mind?"

"Let's just say my opinion isn't as rock solid as it used to be."

"I'll take that for now." Greg was smart enough to quit when he was ahead. Pushing Corrine would have the opposite effect. He'd have to be patient, something he was good at, and let her learn for herself how much effort he put into his livelihood. And he had all summer to accomplish it.

"I travel a lot with my job," he said. "Then *and* now. To recreational spots around the world. It's another reason people think I'm a slacker. Leah abhorred my come-and-go schedule. She wanted stability for her children. Not a dad who popped in twice a year for Christmas and birthdays, or worse, took the kids away."

"But you did. Take them away, that is."

"I did. And she's not happy about it."

The rising sun cut through the tree branches, warming Greg and causing a thin sheen of perspiration to break out on his brow beneath his hat. On second thought, his proximity to Corrine could be the reason. She moved, and her knee brushed his.

"Obtaining joint custody was a battle," he said, getting back on topic and his thoughts on safer ground. "A top-notch attorney and being able to stay here on the ranch for the summer helped convince the judge. I did have to agree that Leah could come visit the kids in July."

"Will she?"

"Count on it. She can't last four hours without calling my cell phone and demanding to talk to them."

"I can understand how hard it must be for her to be separated from them."

"I can, too. But her constant calling doesn't make bonding any easier for the three of us."

"How did you find out they were yours?"

"Pure coincidence. Leah was good friends with another woman in Mom's neighborhood. The friend knew about Ben and Annie, but not that I was their father. Leah had told everyone he was a man she'd met in Denver. She stayed in touch with her friend over the years. Last Christmas, the friend hosted an open house on New Year's Day and invited everyone on the street. Mom stopped by and happened to see one of those holiday photo cards taped to the refrigerator. Ben and Annie do look a lot like me."

"Yes, they do."

"Mom put two and two together and called me. At first, I told her to let it drop. I was sure if the kids were mine, Leah would have come after me for child support long ago. I might have been an unknown when she and I dated, but I've done okay since then, and what mother wouldn't want financial security for her children?"

"Leah, apparently."

Greg nodded. He half hoped Corrine would forget about the thirty minute limit he'd promised her. He was in no hurry to return to the ranch and in no hurry to leave her.

"Mom kept nagging. Once she got it in her head she might be a grandmother, she became a force. And I'm glad she did. As much as I tried to convince myself to forget about Ben and Annie, I couldn't. My dad wasn't the easiest person to get along with. He and I...well, we fought a lot. I didn't want to be like him. If I had children out there, I was going to be an involved father. And a good one." He kicked at a small stone. "I don't think I'm there yet."

"You're trying. Surely Ben and Annie see that."

"Do *you* see it?" Greg glanced toward Corrine, encouraged by the emotional intimacy of their conversation.

"I see an inexperienced man being the best father he knows how to be."

"You think I'm too easy on the kids."

"It makes sense, now that you've explained."

Fishing with Corrine was infinitely more enjoyable than doing so alone. He thought about how he could get her to go with him again. Bring the kids along, as she'd suggested.

"My dad yelled," he said. "Constantly. At me. At my mom. At his employees. He spent twelve hours a day at the office and when he came home, he'd start in on whoever was handiest. My mom and I couldn't make him happy no matter what we did. We lived near a tributary of the Snake River. I'd sneak out and go fishing whenever I could. In the beginning, it was an escape. Eventually, fishing became a passion. I guess I have my dad to thank for one thing."

"He also taught you tolerance and patience by showing you how *not* to behave."

Greg chuckled mirthlessly. "I wasn't always this relaxed. When I was fourteen, I started yelling back at my dad, just as loudly and relentlessly. Our neighbors called us 'the screamers' behind our backs and after a while, to our faces." Greg stood and retrieved his pole, agitated by the direction the conversation had taken. "I refuse to raise Ben and Annie the same way."

"They still need discipline and rules."

"And you know this because you've raised so many children?"

"No, I haven't." She stood in turn. "But I do have a lot of experience managing people."

"Is that why the kitchen is running with the efficiency of a train wreck?"

"It's time to go back."

She had a sore spot, all right, and he'd just found it. Eyes sparking, spine ramrod straight, she spun, swatted at a low-hanging tree branch and marched up the trail toward the golf cart.

There went his idea of spending all summer convincing Corrine of his finer merits.

Greg considered staying at the creek—his easygoing nature came with a stubborn streak—but he'd promised Briana he'd return by lunch. Taking one last look at the boulder he and Corrine had shared, he trudged up the trail after her. Slowly.

She sat in the golf cart, rigid, stoic and uncommunicative.

It wasn't how he'd wanted to end the morning.

Still, as awkward as the outing had ended, he'd go fishing with her over his film crew any old day.

Chapter Five

Corrine exited Jake's office after making her regular afternoon calls, her mood glum. Her phone session had been anything but productive. Highway construction had caused deliveries to be delayed or canceled altogether, the price of produce had risen eight percent in the last week and she'd yet to hire a dishwasher.

Natalie stood behind the front desk. She caught sight of Corrine and abruptly beckoned her over. "These are for you."

Corrine accepted the slips of paper from her outstretched hand with a sinking stomach. Her worst fears were confirmed when she opened and read the first complaint.

"Sorry." A sad smile accompanied Natalie's condolences. "I hated taking them down but…"

"Don't sweat it. You were just doing your job."

"If there's anything I can do to help, give a holler. I'm off work the next two days."

"Thanks," Corrine answered with a coolness she immediately regretted. Natalie was merely the messenger. "I've got everything under control."

Nothing could be further from the truth.

Corrine skimmed the three complaints, about overcooked food, slow service, limited selections and a wheat-free meal not prepared as promised. If the young guest's mother hadn't been paying strict attention, they could have had one very sick boy on their hands, and the finger of blame would have pointed squarely at Corrine.

Had she told Gerrie about the boy's special diet? Corrine couldn't remember. Greg was seriously sabotaging her schedule *and* her concentration. She wished she hadn't gone fishing with him, and not just for herself and her own bruised feelings. The bad note on which their outing had ended wouldn't aid the ranch and her family's cause. They needed Greg happy and satisfied.

If she were completely honest, she'd have to admit that parts of the morning had been kind of nice. Nicer than she'd expected. Then he'd gone and ruined it all by bringing up problems with her staff. Or was it she who had ruined things by criticizing his parenting skills?

"Okay. See you later." Natalie responded to Corrine's dismissal with similar coolness and returned to her work station behind the front desk, chin up, fake smile plastered on her face.

Corrine wanted to kick herself. She hadn't intended to treat her former friend poorly. She'd let her humiliation over the complaints affect her tone and, obviously, her good judgment.

"How's Shiloh?" she asked, attempting to make amends by inquiring after Natalie's fourteen-month-old daughter.

"Growing bigger every day." Natalie must have appreciated Corrine's efforts, weak as they were, for her smile turned genuine. "She's walking now and talking a little."

"Really?"

"Not much. A few words like *dada* and *baba*. Aaron and I figure by next month she'll be saying complete sentences." Natalie hesitated. "You should come by the house one day and see her."

"I'd love to." Corrine held up the stack of complaints and grimaced. "As soon as I stop getting these."

And hired another dishwasher, located a cheaper produce supplier and met with Gerrie about guests' requests for special diets. For one brief moment, Corrine longed for her army days.

"How was fishing this morning? Catch any?"

"I didn't fish. Just Greg. Ah...Mr. Pfitser." His first name had slipped out naturally. She corrected herself only when Natalie's eyebrows shot up.

"He seems really nice."

"He is." *Sometimes.* Corrine had enough wherewithal this time to think before speaking.

"And good-looking."

"I suppose. If you like that type."

"You mean the tall, broad-shouldered, Brad Pitt and Johnny Depp rolled into one, handsome type?"

Yeah, that type. Corrine tried to pull off a casual shrug. Natalie's eyes twinkled with unsuppressed amusement.

Corrine was starting to accept that she was sunk where Greg was concerned, and more than a little smitten. Damn it! Of all the men at the ranch, employed or visiting, it had to be him who made her damaged heart go pitter-patter.

"I'll see you at dinner." She executed a hasty retreat across the lobby before her friend saw through any more of her pretenses.

Yanking open the front door, Corrine rushed outside, nearly trampling Ben, Annie and their ever faithful canine companion. Yipping excitedly, Belle hopped on her back legs and tried to paw through Corrine's pants. Of the trio, she was the only one happy to see her.

"What are you two doing here?"

"Nothing," Ben answered with obvious reservation. His and his sister's small faces were red with exertion.

Corrine noticed he always spoke first. Was that a boy thing? "You're going to have to take Belle back to your cabin. Remember the rules? No dogs allowed in public areas."

She gently pushed the dog down, but not before giving her a quick pat.

"We will. Later." They ducked their heads and tried to cut around her.

"No, now." She sidestepped, thwarting their plan.

Annie tried reasoning. "Daddy told us to bring back a map of the ranch."

At the mention of Greg's name, Corrine's heart immediately launched into that stupid pitter-patter thing. "Where is he?" She scanned the area for any signs of him.

"Back at the cabin." Ben really did resemble his father, right down to the determined set of his jaw.

"The cabin?" Corrine couldn't believe Greg had let two five-year-olds walk that distance alone. It had to be a quarter mile. Not that they were in the middle of nowhere, but still, there were dangers. One of them could have tripped and fallen, or wandered off the trail. The creek was deep enough in parts for a small child to drown in.

"He's working." Annie's tone was mildly defensive.

Could be they liked their father more than he thought they did.

"Working or not, he shouldn't have let you walk all that distance alone."

Corrine wavered. Dinner was being served in less than two hours, and if she didn't want another stack of complaints, she needed to be supervising her staff with the preparations. Taking the kids inside made the most sense. Natalie could watch them until Greg arrived. Surely they had his cell phone number on file.

That wasn't, however, what Corrine did, and no one was more surprised than her.

"I'll take you back in the golf cart."

"We can't go without the map," Ben whined.

"I'll grab one at the front desk when I get the keys." She drew up short. Neither of the twins was trustworthy, and they were likely to run off if she left them outside. "Come with me." She guaranteed their cooperation by relieving Ben of the dog's leash.

As soon as she had the keys in her possession, she led the twins out the main lodge through a rear employee exit. The fewer guests who saw the dog, the better.

Belle was obviously no stranger to vehicles. With minimal coaxing, she hopped into the golf cart and onto the front passenger seat. The same couldn't be said for Ben and Annie. Their uneasiness increased the closer they got to the cabin.

Corrine was too irritated with their father to pay much attention. She still couldn't get over that Greg would not only let his children roam the ranch alone, he'd apparently instructed them to do so. His conduct went beyond inexperienced parenting to downright neglect.

Greg's cabin appeared around the next bend. Belle leaped off the seat the instant they came to a stop, and ran to the door, where she immediately started scratching.

Corrine marched forward, the unfamiliar Toyota parked next to Greg's SUV barely registering. Rather than race inside as she expected, Ben and Annie dallied on the porch. One of them hung on the railing, the other slumped into a metal lawn chair. She raised her hand, intending to rap loudly on the door. A second before her knuckles made contact, it swung open. Belle shot inside. Corrine's jaw went slack, and the reprimand she'd planned on delivering to Greg died on her lips.

"Hello, luv." The greeting was issued by a statuesque blond whose phenomenal curves were stuffed into a midriff-revealing top and short denim skirt, both one size too small. Bracing a forearm on the doorjamb, she slouched seductively and winked at Corrine. "We weren't expecting any company."

"Is, um, Mr. Pfitser available?" Corrine wasn't accustomed to being dwarfed by other women. This one left her feeling inadequate in more ways than she liked.

"Mr. Pfitser?" That smile, big and brassy to begin with, widened. "Ain't we all formal-like?" She gestured for Corrine to enter the cabin.

She wasn't sure she wanted to.

"Come along, luv. I won't bite. Not you, anyway. A dishy bloke, now that's another story."

Ben chose that moment to poke his head around Corrine and gawk, saucer-eyed, at the woman.

She ruffled his hair. "I told you earlier, tiger, you're too young. Even for me."

He tripped over his feet in his haste to scramble backward.

"Men." The woman rolled her eyes before bouncing into the cabin's small living room.

Corrine tentatively placed one foot over the threshold.

"Shut the door, will you? You're letting in the light."

A man's voice. Gruff. Definitely not Greg's. Just what the heck was going on here? For the sake of Ben and Annie, Corrine felt she should find out.

"You two wait here," she told the kids. "Don't leave."

Amazingly, they agreed with a meek "Okay." Whoever these people in Greg's cabin were, they'd taken a little of the edge off Ben's stubbornness and Annie's defensiveness.

Checking on the kids one last time, Corrine entered the darkened cabin and closed the door behind her. Once her vision adjusted, she took a good look around and suppressed a gasp. The place was a certified disaster area, and the mess was adult, not juvenile.

Suitcases and canvas bags were haphazardly stacked in the

middle of the room, blocking the path to the short hallway. One lay open, revealing a pink thong, a pair of binoculars and an accordion file. Aluminum cans, candy wrappers, peanut shells and crumpled napkins littered the furniture and floor. Belle licked at a sticky spot on the corner of the coffee table.

Corrine grimaced, her worry about the twins' welfare reaching new heights.

A man, the same one who'd barked at her to shut the door, sat on the couch. It sagged deeply in the middle beneath his weight. He had a laptop computer open on the coffee table in front of him and was furiously tapping the keys. As she approached, he stopped typing and glanced up. Then did a double take, after which his gaze lingered for several lengthy seconds.

"Hello." This time, his voice was anything but gruff. "And where did you come from, pretty lady?"

"I brought Ben and Annie back."

"They were gone?" He turned a questioning look on the woman, who'd wandered into the tiny kitchenette and stood at the open refrigerator.

"Apparently." Her answer lacked concern. "Anyone care for a refreshment? I'm damn near parched."

"No, thank you." Corrine's frustration and confusion were increasing by the second. "Where's Greg?" She had to wonder if he'd sent the kids away in order to protect them from these two weirdos or to be alone with them.

"Bedroom," the man answered, and pushed himself to his feet.

"Can someone get Greg for me?" Her request came out like an order.

"Sure." He turned his stocky body halfway around and hollered, "Greg!"

"What?" came a muffled reply.

"You have company."

Corrine squared her shoulders and assumed her best commanding officer posture.

The man didn't appear impressed or intimidated. Rather, he seemed to be enjoying himself. Immensely. So did the woman in the kitchen. She'd helped herself to a beer and was relishing it with obvious satisfaction.

Finally, Greg emerged from one of the two bedrooms, his clothing rumpled and his hair disheveled. He clutched a stack of loose papers in his hand and was scratching his head. "I can't find pages three and seven."

"Good luck," the woman in the kitchen said matter-of-factly. "Maybe our visitor can tell us if there's a spare printer at the ranch we can borrow. Ours has decided to run out of toner. Very inconvenient."

His head snapped up. He, too, did a double take when he saw Corrine, only his lingering glance left her a tiny bit breathless.

Camo pants and T-shirts had never affected any of the male soldiers she'd worked with quite the way it did these two. The woman in the kitchen was showing considerably more skin, yet they hardly noticed her. Another one of those annoying tingles skittered up Corrine's spine.

For crying out loud, what was wrong with her? She did not and never had gone gooey inside just because a man deemed to give her an admiring once-over.

No, not any man. Greg.

This really had to stop.

"I brought Ben and Annie back."

He furrowed his brows. "From where? They're playing outside."

"They are now. Ten minutes ago they were at the main lodge. Said you sent them there to get a map of the ranch."

"I sent them to the truck to get the one I'd left on the front seat." He dropped the papers on the nearest available surface space, which happened to be the pile of suitcases and duffel bags. The pink thong disappeared from sight. "Don't go anywhere," he told her. "I'll be right back."

Hadn't she given almost the exact same instructions to Ben and Annie?

Greg went outside, she presumed to talk to the kids and get to the bottom of their misunderstanding. He really had looked confused and upset, causing her to regret her hasty assumption. Greg was certainly guilty of absentmindedness and slovenly housekeeping, but not criminal negligence.

Corrine shifted, feeling the stares of the room's two occupants.

"I'm Russ." The man came forward to shake her hand. "And that's Paulette over there."

"Charmed." The blond beamed.

"Nice to meet you, too," Corrine muttered, still unsure what to make of Greg's friends. "I'm Corrine Sweetwater." She sneaked a discreet peek through the window. How long did reprimanding two five-year-olds take?

Russ's eyes lit up. "The kitchen manager. I should have guessed."

"Did Greg tell you about me?"

"No, the rascal didn't. And we're going to have a long talk about it later. Not that I fault the guy. I'd keep you to myself, too, if I were in his shoes." Russ sat back down and picked through four cans of soda sitting beside his laptop, lifting each one to test its contents. "It was Ben who squealed on you." He lifted a can to his mouth and drained the contents. "He's quite impressed with your cooking."

Ben was probably the only person at Bear Creek Ranch making that claim.

"Do you work for Greg?" Corrine asked.

"We're his crew."

Ah, that explained a lot, including the mess. "When are the rest of you arriving?"

"Paulette and I are it."

"Only the pair of you? To film a television show?"

"I'm the director and cameraman. Paulette's the assistant producer."

"Don't let the fancy title fool you." She came around the kitchen counter to join them in the living room. "On a show this size, assistant producer translates into scriptwriter, equipment manager, makeup artist, hairstylist, wardrobe mistress, talent scout, gopher and anything else we need. Judging by what just happened—" she nodded in the direction of the door "—I might be recruited for nanny duty, too."

Corrine was quickly overcoming her trepidation about these two and finding herself more than a little fascinated.

"We're going to need a few things," Paulette said. "Like that map of the ranch Greg sent the munchkins after. And a wireless Internet connection, as well as access to a land line and directions to the closest office supply store."

"Natalie Forrester, our manager of guest services, should be able to help you with anything you need. If not, my cousin Jake can. He's head manager. I'm only in charge of the kitchen."

"What if I have a special meal request?" Russ asked.

"Are you on a restricted diet?"

"Not exactly. My request was more along the lines of you joining us for dinner."

"I can't. I'm working tonight." Reality returned with blinding force, reminding Corrine that she'd been absent from the dining hall far too long. "Speaking of which, I have to go."

Russ hopped up off the couch. "Need a ride?"

"I have one. Thanks." Smiling, she inched toward the door and made it through. Almost.

Greg was on the other side.

"Oops, sorry." She'd almost clobbered him in her haste. "Are you okay?"

"Fine."

Corrine paused, struck by Greg's demeanor. Mr. Laid-Back looked ready to climb the nearest wall. "You sure?"

He ignored her question. "I didn't send Ben and Annie to the main lodge."

"I realize that."

"Now you do. But you were seeing red when you first arrived."

"As you said, it was a misunderstanding."

"I'd just checked on them a few minutes earlier. Or thought I did. It's been crazy since Russ and Paulette arrived."

Corrine would give him that. "They probably weren't gone long. I think they ran the whole way to the main lodge." She started to squeeze past him.

He stopped her with a hand on her shoulder. The other one he used to shut the cabin door.

And just like that, they were alone.

Ben and Annie were playing behind the cabin. Corrine could hear their voices. She could also hear Russ's and Paulette's muffled conversation on the other side of the door. So close, yet she and Greg might as well have been a thousand miles away.

His hand moved off her shoulder and down her arm. Corrine tensed, then melted when his fingertips encountered the sensitive skin of her forearm. The temptation to shut her eyes and lean into him was almost too strong to resist. He didn't help matters by narrowing the space separating them to a teeny-tiny two inches.

For one crazy, impulsive second, she thought he meant to kiss her. Corrine didn't have to ask herself what she'd do in response. Her lips were already parted in anticipation, and her arms itched to loop around his neck.

"I'd like to return the favor," he said, his breath combining with the mild summer breeze to tickle the fine hairs at her temple.

Here it comes. He was going to ask her out. Suggest dinner and a movie, or to go dancing at the local country-and-western honky-tonk. Her befuddled brain scrambled for a polite way to refuse. It was a waste of mental energy. Whatever he suggested, she'd accept.

"You don't have to."

"Yes, I do." He reached up to cup her cheek.

Sighing softly, she lifted her face to meet his kiss.

"I'll come by the kitchen right after dinner."

She blinked. "Tonight?" That was fast.

"And tomorrow, too, if you need me."

"Need you?" Corrine wanted to go out with him but she wasn't *that* desperate for a date.

"I thought you were still short a dishwasher."

"I am, but—"

"I'll help. I owe you for today, and it's the least I can do."

Help washing dishes? Corrine wanted to kick herself. She'd completely misread Greg's signals. Doing a fair imitation of Ben stumbling over his own feet, she backed away and fled to the golf cart.

"Corrine, wait!" He came after her.

She jammed the vehicle into Reverse and floored the gas.

It was only when she reached the kitchen that she remembered she'd forgotten to decline his offer of help.

Chapter Six

"See you tomorrow," Gerrie said on her way out the door. She was the last of the kitchen staff to leave.

Corrine stopped her hasty exit by asking, "How's the egg supply?" Guests had vacated the dining room only an hour earlier, and already she was anticipating the next morning's breakfast.

"Enough to last us till Friday."

"Did Luke prep the cinnamon rolls?"

"Four big pans. They're in the fridge."

"The boy with the wheat intolerance—"

"I have it covered," Gerrie said irritably. "He's getting scrambled eggs, bacon and rice cereal with fresh fruit."

Well, she didn't have it covered yesterday.

Corrine told herself she wasn't wrong to double-check on her assistant cook, and Gerrie had no call to be angry. They were both doing their jobs. It just seemed to Corrine that she cared more about hers than anyone else did theirs.

She shut the pantry door. "Okay. Have a nice night."

"You'll be in at the regular time tomorrow morning?"

"Yes. Absolutely. Six o'clock sharp." No side trips with Greg again. Corrine would placate Jake and do her part making Greg's stay pleasant, but in other ways.

Her worry that he might actually show up to help with the dishes and, God forbid, mention her ridiculous behavior on his front porch that afternoon, had caused her to be short with the staff during dinner service, and unusually demanding.

It occurred to her as she stood in the center of the deserted kitchen that the horrendous mess left for her to clean might have been done on purpose.

Both sinks overflowed with greasy pans and dirty dishes. Grayish grunge stuck to the counters. Containers of perishables sat uncovered and unrefrigerated. Her shoes made crunching noises when she walked. Whatever had spilled on the stove had hardened to the consistency of cement and would require a hammer and chisel to remove.

Corrine had a right to be angry at her staff. While they'd worked diligently to get dinner out the door and on the tables, they hadn't cleaned as they went, one of the cardinal rules of any commercial kitchen.

Retying her loose apron, Corrine flipped on the hot water spigot, added a liberal amount of dish soap and adjusted the sprayer. Analyzing the ulterior motives of her team wouldn't clean the kitchen any faster. It wouldn't boost her sagging morale, either.

Warm steam floated up from the sink, momentarily blurring her vision. She wiped at her eyes with the back of a damp hand. The urge to cry overwhelmed her, and she lost the battle.

Surrendering to her emotions wasn't something Corrine did. As a female officer competing against men for a position of authority, she'd developed a tough as nails exterior. No room for tears in the army. Not if she'd wanted respect and obedience from her subordinates, cooperation from her peers and approval from her commanding officer.

Hector had figured out she had a tender side soon after being assigned to her command, and had tapped into it. Repeatedly. But he'd never broadcasted her weakness around base, which had earned him her trust and her friendship and, ultimately, her deep affection.

Unfortunately, her tender side and his taking advantage of it had also cost him his life.

"Wow. I didn't realize feeding two hundred people made such a mess."

Corrine froze.

Greg! He'd come, after all. Thank goodness she had her back to him.

Grabbing the neck band of her T-shirt, she used it to wipe her face and erase any signs of her crying jag. "You're here," she said, and grimaced at the telltale huskiness in her voice.

"Sorry I'm late. I had to go over a few things with Russ and Paulette for tomorrow."

"Where are the kids?"

"With them. Helping move all their luggage and equipment to their cabins."

"I'm glad the reservation snafu got straightened out."

"Ben wasn't keen on the idea of Paulette babysitting. I think she scares him. I bribed him with the promise of another one of those oatmeal cookies from dinner."

Corrine heard the debris crunching beneath Greg's shoes as he approached. She bit her bottom lip. *Not yet. Please. Just give me three more seconds to pull myself together.*

He didn't. "Are you all right?" He'd materialized beside her and was gazing down at her. Then he placed a comforting hand on her shoulder.

Her legs wobbled, and her tenuously held control threatened to collapse. "I'm fine." *Whatever you say, don't bring up this afternoon.* She used the excuse of lifting the dome on the commercial dishwasher to put some much needed space between them.

"You don't look fine. Your face is red and blotchy."

"It's the steam from the hot water."

He appeared to accept her explanation. "There's a lot of dirty dishes here."

"More so than usual."

"Complicated meals tonight?"

"No, complicated staff."

"I don't get it."

She moved to the island and gathered a tub of dinnerware left there by the busers. "We're supposed to clean as we go. I think I'm the only one who did."

He followed her lead and carried a second tub over to the counter. "Sounds like sabotage to me."

"More like mutiny. But I really can't be mad." Talking to Greg about her problems with her staff wasn't hard at all, not like with her cousin Jake, and the more she talked, the less she felt like crying. *Strange.* "I kind of bailed on them yesterday and today."

"Ouch! I shouldn't have monopolized your time."

"It's not your fault. A manager should be able to take a few hours off without the whole place falling apart. I could, too, if I were better organized." She didn't mention her inadequacies as kitchen manager. That revelation was too personal and not one she was ready to discuss with anyone.

"You'll get there. You only left the army, what? six weeks ago?"

"Almost two months."

"Don't be so hard on yourself."

She shrugged. "Personnel problems like the ones I'm having don't exist in the army. If a staff member didn't cut it, one phone call and they were reassigned. Their replacement reported for duty by the next meal service. No ads, no interviews, no preemployment drug testing and background checks." Caught up in her complaint, she rambled on. "You won't believe what happened today. This student called about the opening, and when I mentioned how much the job pays, he wanted to negotiate a benefits package." She slapped her forehead. "For a dishwasher position."

"Well, what can I do to help?"

"How are you at scrubbing an oven top?"

"I did mention I'm not much of a housekeeper."

"All you really need is a lot of elbow grease."

"I can manage that." He flexed his arm.

No doubt about it, Greg sported some pretty impressive muscles. Corrine had worked side by side with her share of well-built men, but none of them had made the prospect of close teamwork so appealing...and so nerve-racking.

AFTER A ROCKY START, Corrine and Greg found their rhythm. He asked her all sorts of questions about her stint in the service, which she was slow to answer. When he asked her why she didn't re-up, she changed the subject.

"My cousin Jake has your book. He ordered it online after he and your agent finalized the arrangements for the tournament."

"Did he like it?" Greg had finished with the stove top and was mopping the floor.

"He did. Honestly. I'm thinking of borrowing the book my next full day off."

"You won't need a full day. It's not exactly heavy reading. More like a journal of my adventures on the professional fishing circuit. The good, the bad, the funny and the scary."

"What's scary about fishing?"

"You'd be surprised." He went to the laundry sink in the rear of the kitchen and rinsed the mop. "I'll have you know I've run for my life on several occasions."

"Right." She smirked.

"Honestly. Once, near Vancouver, I picked the wrong

stream to fish in for salmon. Someone was already there and not happy to see me and my film crew."

"Who was it?"

"Not who. What. An eight-hundred-pound grizzly bear."

"Oh, my gosh! Did you get out safely? Well, of course you did—you're here. But what happened?"

"We escaped with only one casualty." He paused for effect. "We lost Russ's camera bag."

She groaned at his joke and her susceptibility to it. After a comfortable lull, she asked, "Besides fishing, traveling, fame and fortune, what do you enjoy most about your job?"

Greg laughed. "What else is there?" He was beside her again at the sink, and like that morning when they'd shared the boulder, body parts brushed and touched. Was there any mundane activity this man didn't make sexy just by bumping into her?

He deposited a fistful of utensils in the sink.

"Seriously," she prompted, ignoring the rush of awareness that coursed through her when their fingers briefly tangled.

"I'm a ham at heart. I love being in front of the camera."

"Really?"

"You clearly haven't watched *Fishing with Pfitser.*"

"No, I haven't, but don't take offense. Other than the news, I don't watch much TV."

"I understand. I don't watch much myself. Unless you count the cartoon network. Ben and Annie are addicted."

"You'd be surprised at the number of soldiers who like cartoons. I think the silliness takes their minds off the horrors they witness. I had a friend—" She stopped and swallowed. Greg was the first nonmilitary person she'd talked to about Hector, and she did so only because he gave her space by leaving the sink to unplug the coffee urns. "His name was Hector. He loved the X-Men."

Corrine found herself battling for control again.

"What do you like best about your job?" Greg asked.

He was washing out the coffee urns and didn't appear to notice her distress.

"The structure. The army is nothing if not regimented. And the camaraderie. All of us had a mission, the same one, and were dedicated to achieving it."

"I meant, what do you like about *this* job?"

"Oh." She faltered. "I don't know. I haven't been at it very long."

In that moment, she envied Greg. He loved what he did and made a good living at it. Everyone should be so lucky.

Greg had definitely underestimated his housekeeping skills. In less time than Corrine would have guessed possible, they'd loaded the last of the dirty dinnerware and were scrubbing out the empty sinks. Thanks to him, Corrine was actually going to hit the sack at a decent hour tonight.

More than his help, she'd enjoyed his company. He'd let her vent about her problems without offering criticism or solutions, and he'd distracted her with conversation. In short, he'd been a friend. Her first one since Hector died.

"Thank you," she told Greg, closing up the pantry.

"Am I hired?"

Gathering the mountain of soiled towels, she threw them and their aprons into the laundry hamper. "I wish. But I can't afford you."

He wheeled the bucket to the laundry sink and dumped the dirty mop water. "I work cheap, and I don't need a benefit package."

"Not that cheap."

He grinned. "Maybe you could sweeten the pot."

"How's that?" She turned off all the lights save one over the now gleaming stovetop, and began walking toward him in the semidarkness. Her gait was slow, like his, but for different reasons.

With one shoulder braced on the doorjamb, Greg oozed an impossible-to-resist sex appeal. "I'm sure we can come up with something if we put our heads together."

There it was again—that change of tone in his voice, from casual to seductive. He sounded just like he had that afternoon at his cabin when she'd misread his signals and almost made a fool of herself.

Careful, she cautioned herself.

"Are you referring to those oatmeal cookies from dinner you promised Ben?"

She was being purposely obtuse. They were too close, the room too dark and the sexual undercurrents too strong for her to give Greg the slightest indication that she was receptive to his flirting. If she let her guard down even a little, he might take advantage of her.

And she might let him.

The resulting fireworks would be enough to light up the night sky from the ranch to Payson.

"What do you think I'm referring to?"

They stood facing each other in front of the door. Neither so much as lifted a finger to open it. "Something other than cookies," she said in a whisper.

"You're right."

They were within easy reaching distance. Greg proved it by wrapping an arm around her waist and hauling her against his very hard, exceedingly fine chest. No mistaking signals this time. She didn't resist his embrace. She was too busy standing on her tiptoes and seeking his mouth with hers to put up a protest.

Her lips parted the moment they made contact with his. For a man with a reputation of doing everything at half speed, he moved quickly. Before she quite realized what was happening, he'd backed her up and pinned her to the wall. The last man to try a move like that had wound up eating dirt. But this wasn't a combat drill, and Greg wasn't her opponent. She welcomed his long, lean body into her arms and returned his hot, hungry kisses with equal fervor.

Seconds stretched into minutes. Corrine was in no hurry to come to her senses. For all her tough exterior, she was pure woman on the inside. Responding to Greg's male advances felt not only natural, it felt right. Groaning, he lowered his hands to cup her hips and fit her more snugly between him and the wall. She shifted, improving their alignment to bone-melting perfection.

Returning to civilian life had suddenly taken on a whole new meaning.

Which was why, when he abruptly pulled back and ended the kiss, she didn't quite believe it.

"I heard a noise," he said, his breath ragged.

She heard it, too. A loud clatter.

"What's that?"

"A raccoon, I think." They were still locked together, and her arms remained looped around his neck. "Sneaking into the trash Dumpster."

"Should we do something?"

"He'll leave when we do."

Greg's cell phone rang. He removed it from his belt, retreated a step and checked the caller ID. "Great."

The real world, gone the instant he had drawn her into his embrace, came crashing down. "Trouble?" she asked.

"Yes." He flipped open the phone and, frowning, put it to his ear. "Hello, Leah."

Since the kids weren't there for her to speak to, Greg's conversation with his ex was short and clipped. Corrine didn't need to hear both sides to know that Leah wasn't happy about his choice of babysitters. His face conveyed the full extent of her impatience and his annoyance. He ended with a promise to have the kids return her call within the next fifteen minutes, just to prove they were alive and unharmed.

"Sorry," he said, disconnecting.

"No problem." Corrine pushed away from the wall.

Picking up where they'd left off wasn't an option. The mood had vanished with the ringing of Greg's cell phone. It really was for the best. They'd gotten a little carried away.

More than a little, Corrine thought, running a finger across her moist lips. The taste of Greg and the sensation of his muscular form molded to hers came rushing back to her. Both impressions would be imprinted on her memory forever.

"We'd better go," she said, removing the kitchen keys from her pocket.

"Yeah." Greg didn't look happy. "Can I give you a ride to your cabin?" he asked. "I brought the SUV."

"It's only a five minute walk." She'd been bunking with her older sister, Carolina, since returning to the ranch.

"We're filming in the morning. Would you like to come watch?"

They'd reached the end of the parking lot, and she came to a halt. "I'm working."

"I'll see you at breakfast then."

"Maybe."

"Ow!" He winced. "These brush-offs really smart."

"Greg."

He held up a hand. "No awkward regrets. Please. I don't have any and you shouldn't, either."

"I don't. But I also think a reevaluation is wise right about now."

The sun had set about an hour earlier, and lights glittered all over the ranch. If Corrine and Greg were lovers, the view would be perfect for a romantic moonlight stroll. Only they weren't lovers. In truth, they were hardly more than strangers.

"Why?" he asked.

"For starters, you're leaving in less than six weeks. I'm not interested in anything…short-term." Until she fully recovered from losing Hector, she wasn't sure she'd be ready for any relationship, short- or long-term.

"Things change. Who knows what can happen in six weeks?" He reached up and tucked a strand of hair behind her ear. She was almost tempted to float into his arms again.

Definitely no regrets about kissing him. In fact, if she—

With a jolt, Corrine realized just how vulnerable she was to Greg's charms and how cautious she'd have to be around him, or risk losing her head and heart. A step back seemed in order.

"We each have responsibilities. Me to my job and my family, you to your job and your children. Spending time with them is the whole reason you came here. I don't want to come between you and them."

"I hate that you're right."

"Good night, Greg."

Feeling they were left with no other choice but to put a firm end to what they'd started, she turned and headed down the road toward her sister's cabin.

Chapter Seven

"Four, three, two, one and action!"

Greg stared into the camera with its blinking red light and tried to remember his lines. They didn't come.

"I said 'action'," Russ repeated.

Stalling for time, Greg stepped onto the small footbridge. The moment his hand made contact with the railing, Russ started moving backward down the bridge and onto a densely wooded trail. Amazingly, he didn't trip. Greg often kidded his director about having eyes in the back of his head, but then, exceptional skills were a requirement for anyone in Russ's profession. Cameras cost a small fortune. An accidental dunk in the river could render equipment inoperable and bring a budget conscious show like Greg's to a grinding halt.

"We're here at Bear Creek Ranch, situated on the southern rim of Arizona's pine country. It's to this picturesque spot that fishermen from all over the country come to enjoy some of the state's best trout fishing—"

"Cut!" Russ turned off the camera, eased it down from his shoulder and gaped at Greg as if he didn't recognize him. "What the hell was that? You sounded as if you were reading a brochure."

Busted. He had, in fact, used the copy from one he'd picked up at the front desk. "I was improvising. We lost that page from the script, remember?"

"What you said was not improvising. Let's try again."

Belle yipped, and Greg automatically turned to check on Ben and Annie. His heart jumped into overdrive.

"Kids, no. Get down from there." They'd climbed an oak tree. Only to where the trunk formed a Y, but high enough to agitate Belle and give Greg visions of a trip to the emergency room, complete with stitches and casts. "Now, please."

Reluctantly, they complied.

"Thank you, guys."

"We're bored," Ben complained, digging at the ground with a stick. "We want to go swimming."

The pool had been off-limits since their minor mishap the other day.

"We will. This afternoon." If Greg ever got done with this shoot.

"I thought you hired someone to watch them," Russ grumbled. He was the father of three and liked having children around, but not while working.

"The company flaked at the last minute."

"Find someone else."

"I have. The manager's daughter. But she's not available twenty-four/seven."

"Well, maybe you need someone who is."

Russ was right. They'd been at it for an hour already this morning, and had shot hardly any usable footage. Ben and Annie weren't intentionally causing trouble. They were just active, rambunctious and curious five-year-olds who required constant supervision.

"There's nothing I can do about a babysitter this morning."

The instant they were done, Greg intended to visit Jake's assistant, Alice, and seek her help. He also considered asking Corrine for the contact information to the college. One of the students attending summer school might be in need of a part-time job with flexible hours.

Thinking of Corrine reminded him of the previous night and their kiss. Make that kisses, as in multiple. Once he'd gotten a taste of her, stopping had been damn near impossible. Her enthusiastic participation, along with the instantaneous surge of passion that had flared between them, was both unexpected and incredible. In a matter of seconds, she'd reduced him from a man in control to one completely at her mercy.

If she didn't hire a new dishwasher today, he'd be reporting for duty again. Forget wages. He'd work for the perks alone.

"Ready?" Russ hollered.

"Yeah."

Greg shook his head to clear it, resumed his place on the footbridge and adjusted his trademark hat. Ben's and Annie's antics weren't the only reasons for him forgetting his lines. Corrine was equally responsible. Greg didn't think he'd be shaking either distraction anytime soon.

Russ called for action again.

"Folks, I'm here today to let you in on a well-kept secret. Bear Creek Ranch." Greg gestured with his arm, flashed his most winning smile and concentrated on getting into the zone. "Here, for only a few months during the spring and summer, you can enjoy some of the best, most exciting trout fishing in the entire western United States."

Finally, he was feeling it. Lines from the script Paulette had written came back to him, and he recited them for the camera, adding a joke or two of his own. Good. Everything was flowing. Russ was motioning with his hand, signaling that he liked what he saw. Another minute. Another dozen lines and they'd be done with this shot. Happy day!

In the next instant, everything *stopped* flowing and went to hell in a handbasket. Belle lunged into the creek, making a huge commotion. Ben charged in after her and Annie after him, the two of them hollering at the top of their lungs for the dog to come back. Water splashed everywhere.

Greg didn't think. He dropped his fishing pole, vaulted over the bridge railing and landed feetfirst in the shallow creek. "Ben! Annie!"

Russ went nuts. "Cut! Cut!" He lowered the camera and curled his body protectively around it. And not a moment too soon. Belle sprang from the creek and chose Russ's feet as the ideal spot to shake herself dry.

Greg reached Annie first, then Ben. He grabbed them both, his instinct to protect them overriding everything else.

"What are you doing?" he cried.

"Belle ran away," Ben answered.

"That's no reason for you to jump in the creek."

They were trembling and looking at him as if he might chew their heads off.

Greg saw the face of his five-year-old self reflected in theirs, heard his father's angry tone in his own voice, and went cold inside. He wasn't his father, and he didn't strong-arm his children.

Standing knee-deep in water, he pulled Ben and Annie to his sides. "I'm sorry. I shouldn't have yelled at you."

They hugged him back. Hesitantly at first, then fiercely. Emotions filled Greg's chest, unbearably sweet and wretchedly painful as the past mingled with the present.

"It won't happen again. I promise." He gave their tiny shoulders another reassuring squeeze. "Let's get out of here, okay?"

"Look at Belle." Annie pointed to the dog, who was rolling on the ground, all four paws waving in the air. When she stood up, she was covered with dried grass and bits of leaves.

"Looks like we're all going to need a good bath." Greg lifted the children and carried them, one in each arm, to the bank, where he set them down. They could have walked, but he wasn't ready to let go of them. Not yet. For the last four months he'd been a father, but he hadn't really felt like one until right now.

"We'll pick this up in an hour," he said to Russ, then patted Ben on the back. "Why don't you go get Belle? And use the bridge this time, buddy, okay?"

Both twins took off running, their small faces alight with laughter. Greg's chest swelled yet again, with another, more powerful emotion. Who knew parenting could be such fun?

Russ's thundering footsteps on the bridge put a swift end to Greg's father-and-children moment.

"Where the hell are you going?"

"Watch your language," Greg barked, tilting his head at Ben and Annie.

"Trust me, they've heard worse at preschool."

"I don't care. They're not hearing it from you."

"You can't leave. We don't have a single decent shot."

"One hour."

"Do I need to remind you of just how tight our schedule is?"

"I know." Greg had put the show behind when he'd chosen to remain a few extra days in Denver with the kids rather than whisk them straight away to the ranch. He didn't regret his decision despite the added pressure he'd caused his crew. "We'll double up this afternoon."

"Like that's going to happen. Unless you find a sitter between now and then."

"I'll figure something out."

"Greg, Greg, Greg," Russ intoned. "This playing daddy is great stuff, man. I support you one hundred percent. But there's a time and a place, and this ain't it. You don't see me dragging any of my three holy terrors to work."

Ben returned from retrieving Belle, with Annie hovering behind him. The two eyed Greg with the same stark uncertainty they had most of the last few months. He didn't like it. Not after the closeness they'd shared only minutes before.

"And what about the tournament?" Russ said. "It's five weeks away."

"I haven't forgotten."

"You might consider sending the kids home early. Like tomorrow."

"That's enough, Russ!" Greg instantly lowered his voice, afraid of upsetting Ben and Annie. "We'll talk about this later."

"We will, pal. And I think Irene should be on it."

There was only one reason Russ would want to involve Greg's agent—to drum some sense into him.

Greg took Ben and Annie by their small hands. "Give me another day before you call in the reserves." His children weren't returning to Denver until the end of summer, not if he could help it.

He was developing a real appreciation of what Leah went through. Being a single working parent wasn't easy. It must have taken a lot of courage for her to decide to raise Ben and Annie on her own. And if what she felt for them was anything close to what he did, being separated from them must be sheer torture.

The next time she called demanding to speak to the kids, Greg was determined to be more understanding. It might make their joint parenting go more smoothly.

He wouldn't, however, discuss his child care dilemma with her. Newly discovered understanding aside, it would be just like Leah to try and overturn the judge's decision to grant them shared custody. Especially if she had the slightest indication he wasn't coping well.

"How is everything tonight?" Corrine cruised by the tables, stopping and chatting with guests. "Did you get enough shrimp cocktail? Thank you, and no, I can't tell. The salad dressing is a secret family recipe."

To her relief, the comments were generally good. Guests were either satisfied or at least not willing to complain to her face. She hoped it was the former. She didn't need another day like yesterday, in more ways than one.

Steeling her resolve, she readied herself to visit Greg's table, having saved it for last. Russ and Paulette were with him, along with his children, Corrine's parents and an older couple celebrating their fortieth anniversary.

The ranch frequently hosted guests marking significant milestones in their lives—birthdays, graduations, reunions and, of course, honeymoons. Corrine's mother co-owned an antique shop in town, but was also their wedding coordinator. And she kept it in the family. Besides her eldest daughter's wedding, Millie had also helped arrange Jake and Lilly's not so long ago.

"Hi. Is everything satisfactory?" Corrine asked.

"Delicious." Russ appeared to have an appetite similar to Ben's. They'd both consumed enough shrimp cocktail for three people.

"Thank you for personally fixing Annie's dinner." Greg smiled up at Corrine.

"You're welcome." Heat invaded her middle, then crept up to her cheeks when his gaze caught hers and lingered.

She'd purposely remained in the kitchen during breakfast and lunch in the hopes of avoiding him, for just this reason. Seeing him, conversing with him, brought back memories of their indiscreet, if not downright indecent, behavior in the kitchen last night. Not that she hadn't been thinking about it all day. What if Jake had walked in on them? Or an employee returning to retrieve a forgotten item? Being part owner of the ranch wouldn't have spared her from being the center of gossip.

"Where'd you learn to cook?" Russ asked between mouthfuls. "I spent three years as a seaman in the navy and never ate this good."

"Here."

"I bet she wasn't more than fourteen when she started working in the kitchen." Millie smiled fondly, giving away more information than Corrine would have preferred, but then, her mother was a talker. "She took over when our former kitchen manager retired a few weeks ago."

"Well, she left the kitchen in capable hands," Russ said with a satisfied grunt.

Corrine wished it was true. Olivia had been ten times the manager she was.

"How many people usually stay here?" Russ's interest appeared genuine.

Millie loved nothing better than a fresh pair of ears, and talking about the ranch. "We can accommodate a little over two hundred, though our average number of guests is less." She didn't mention how much less that number was lately. "We're hoping to be booked to full capacity during the tournament."

"Macaroni and cheese is my favorite." Annie spoke so softly Corrine barely heard her over the adults.

"Is it?"

She'd reserved a single serving of plain pasta from the enormous batch they'd cooked up tonight for turkey tetrazzini, and used it to make macaroni and cheese. She'd told herself she was simply accommodating a guest's finicky tastes, and that she would have done it for anyone. The fact the guest was Greg's daughter was irrelevant.

Too bad she didn't believe her own lame argument.

From the barely concealed amusement glinting in Greg's eyes, he didn't believe her, either.

Dang it. Just what she needed. Him thinking she was trying to get to him through his daughter.

They really should talk. Last night had been a mistake, the result of overactive hormones and underactive brain cells. It had also been phenomenal and earth-shattering, much to her dismay. She contemplated how best to approach him.

"I'll see you after dinner," he said.

"What for?" Had he read her mind?

"Washing dishes. I owe you, remember."

"Oh, that's not necessary. You already paid me back."

"For yesterday. Not today and the macaroni and cheese."

Everyone at the long, family-style table stopped eating to stare at them, including the older couple.

"I don't know about you—" Paulette grinned mischievously at her dining companions "—but I'm beginning to think nine's a crowd."

"Me, too," Russ answered dejectedly.

"You dog, you're married," she scolded.

"There's no law against fantasizing."

"Yeah," the older man concurred, staring unabashedly at Paulette's spectacular cleavage.

His wife elbowed him hard in the ribs.

Corrine's father had the good sense to glance away before he earned an elbow ribbing, too.

Corrine was flustered. Rather than let them see her discomfort, she chose a graceful exit.

"If you'll excuse me, I have to return to the kitchen."

"Bye." Annie looked shyly up from her plate. "And thanks."

"Anytime." Corrine's reserve melted a little.

Annie really was a sweet kid when she wanted to be. And Ben wasn't so bad, either. Just full of spit and vinegar. Jake had been like that, too, when he was young.

"Good night, everyone."

"See you after dinner," Greg said.

Her feet stuck to the floor. Damn, he wasn't going to give up. "Really, you don't have to help with the dishes. It was my pleasure to prepare Annie's favorite meal."

"I'll help," the older man offered, and earned himself another rib jabbing.

Millie laughed. "We don't expect our guests to work for their keep. We'll help Corrine."

"What about the Leighs' wedding rehearsal?" her father asked. "It's at six-thirty."

Millie made a face. "That's right."

"Why don't *I* lend assistance?" Paulette rose and, before anyone could raise an objection, linked arms with Corrine and swept her from the dining room to the kitchen.

She didn't want Paulette's help any more than Greg's, but refused to make a scene in front of a hundred and fifty diners. Besides, all things considered, it was the lesser of two evils.

She changed her mind, however, once they were in the kitchen, and Paulette said, "Isn't this marvelous? Now we two can have ourselves a lovely chat."

IT WAS LIKE DÉJÀ VU. For the second night in a row, a guest filled the vacant dishwasher position.

"Hmm…" Paulette sorted through the array of identical aprons hanging on the wall beside the pantry. She finally chose one, folded the bib inside and tied it low on her waist, leaving a wide expanse of unprotected bare midriff.

"Afraid not, *luv*." Corrine wagged a finger at Paulette's middle.

"Do I have to?" She batted innocent blue eyes.

"The bib. It's a rule. You can't work in the kitchen if you don't wear proper protection."

"Fiddlesticks." Paulette fussed a bit with the apron, then asked, "Is there a mirror handy?"

What had Corrine been thinking? Anyone who cared more about her appearance than soiling her clothes or injuring herself lacked the right stuff for a dishwasher.

"In the restroom. At the end of the hall." She refrained from muttering under her breath until the door closed. If Jake got wind of this, her head would be on the chopping block for sure. If only she wasn't understaffed...!

Evidently satisfied, Paulette reemerged a minute later and asked, "Where do I start?"

"At the sink. Don't touch anything hot, sharp or plugged in. Understand?"

"Yes, ma'am." She saluted.

"And wear these." Corrine tossed her a pair of rubber gloves. "Don't take them off until I tell you to."

Unlike the previous night, several members of the kitchen staff were still on duty. Their reactions to Paulette varied. Gerrie seethed. Pat and some of the others suppressed giggles. Luke transformed into a blundering, incompetent butterfingers, unable to take his eyes off the assistant producer.

As their respective shifts ended, the staff left, boxing up their dinners to take home rather than eating in the outdoor dining area behind the kitchen, as was tradition back in Olivia Hernandez's day.

Except for Luke. "I can stay if you want me to."

It figured that tonight would be the one time he volunteered for overtime.

Corrine didn't get mad. She appreciated Luke's help regardless of what motivated him. With three of them working instead of two, they'd be able to finish that much faster. Luke's presence also spared her from being alone with Paulette.

"I've worked with Greg for three years now. Since his first show."

Though she hadn't inquired, Corrine listened intently to

Paulette chatter on about Greg. Luke also hung on her every word, but for different reasons.

"He's wonderful," Paulette said, wringing out a dishrag. "Professional, dedicated and a genuinely nice chap."

"I'm sure."

"He's nuts about those kids and absolutely committed to being a good father."

"Uh-huh." Corrine kept her responses to a minimum in an attempt to disguise her fascination.

"He's unattached at the moment, not that there's any short-age of available women. There never is with good-looking, successful men, if you get my drift."

Corrine did, and reduced her minimal response to a lengthy silence. Hearing about Greg and his children was one thing, hearing about his romances quite another. She wished now she'd put Paulette on trash detail instead of Luke. Handing her another bag to go to the Dumpster would provide a convenient end to their conversation.

On the upside, at least Luke was out of earshot. She could do without him hearing the nitty-gritty on her love life.

Wait! Love life? Where had that slip come from? There was nothing remotely akin to love going on between her and Greg, and no potential for it, either.

Setting aside more trash for Luke to dispose of, she straightened and rubbed her forehead. The night had taken on a surreal quality, and she couldn't wait for it to end. Who would be helping her with the dishes tomorrow night? Russ? Ben and Annie? The older couple?

"There's a girl in production. She—"

"I really don't care about Greg's relationships with other women," Corrine interrupted. "Past or present."

Paulette's laughter was as bold and brassy as her smile. "You should be, my dear," she said, loading dinnerware into the commercial dishwasher with surprising ease and efficiency. "You're the first girl he's taken a fancy to in ages."

"You're misreading the situation."

"Oh, I think not."

Luke came inside, and Corrine couldn't pass him another bag of trash fast enough. Paulette grinned at him, and the poor boy promptly tripped over his own feet.

Was *she* among the string of women interested in good-looking and successful Greg? Corrine didn't care. That annoying twinge in her side was indigestion and nothing more.

"He's such a scrumptiously sweet fellow," Paulette cooed. She'd moved on to sorting flatware.

"Nice, yes. But I haven't seen Greg's scrumptious side yet." Unless Corrine counted those very sweet, very scrumptious kisses he'd given her the previous night. The ones right before the steamy, sexy, toes-curling-inside-her-shoes kisses.

"I was referring to your kitchen helper, Luke." Paulette smiled triumphantly.

If the woman wasn't such an incredible worker, Corrine would find an excuse to send her on her way. Paulette should add ace dishwasher to the list of job duties she'd recited the day before. She was remarkably skilled, living proof of the saying looks could be deceiving.

"All kidding aside," she said, scrubbing the last huge pot, "Greg's a darling fellow."

"When he's not being an insufferable pain in the rear." Corrine slapped a wet rag down onto the counter.

Paulette couldn't stop laughing.

Luke returned from a third trip to the Dumpster, and Corrine promptly shut up. The trio made quick work of cleaning the kitchen, thank goodness. Any minute now Corrine's ordeal would be over.

"Can I give you a ride?" Corrine wasn't wild about the idea of extending her 'lovely chat' with Paulette, but neither would she shirk her responsibilities as one-eighth owner of the ranch by refusing to escort a lone woman guest back to her cabin.

"I'll take her," Luke blurted.

"No, that's okay."

"I'd love a ride." Paulette sashayed over to him and pinched his peach-fuzz-covered chin.

He practically went into spasms. "I'll pull my car around. Wait here."

"On pins and needles, luv."

Corrine followed Paulette to the back door and said in a low voice, "He's just eighteen."

"Gawd bless. Don't be such a mother hen. I'm only going to let him drive me to my cabin. Not molest him."

Corrine relaxed. "Still, it might be better if I took you home."

"Naw. You're busy."

"I'm not."

"Yes, you are." Paulette pointed out the window over the sink. A knowing smile played on her lips. "Speaking of scrumptiously sweet fellows, there's one now."

Corrine peered past Paulette's shoulder. A single, low-wattage bulb illuminated the half-dozen scarred and weathered picnic tables. A man sat at the one closest to the kitchen, his features obscured by shadows. No matter. Corrine didn't need light. Her heart immediately recognized the shape of his wide shoulders, his athletic, lean form and the long legs sticking out from under the bench seat.

Greg.

"A word of caution," Paulette said. "Proceed carefully."

"I have no intentions of getting hurt."

"Not you. Him." Her voice lost its friendly lilt. "He's more vulnerable than he appears. You know he lost his father when he was just a lad."

"No, I didn't."

"Heart attack."

"That's too bad."

"Greg blames himself."

"For his father's heart attack?"

"He used to have quite a temper in those days."

"Greg?" That was news.

"He said he got it from his father. The two of them went at it quite regularly. One day, in the middle of a particularly ugly row, his dad keeled over."

"That's awful!"

"Indeed. Of course, it wasn't Greg's fault. The man had a congenital heart condition, aggravated by stress and overwork. But try telling that to a seventeen-year-old racked with guilt. It changed his life."

Corrine sympathized. She knew firsthand how feeling responsible for someone's death could profoundly affect a person.

"Is that why he doesn't yell at his children?"

"Yes, and why he's so laid-back. He refused to be like his dad."

If Corrine had before, she no longer doubted Paulette's relationship with Greg. She wasn't one of those women standing in line for him. She was his friend, and a good one.

"Thanks for telling me. It explains a lot."

"He's a fine man. He deserves a woman who appreciates him and won't take advantage of his easygoing nature."

"No worries. I'm not in the market for a fling."

"Don't get me wrong." Paulette's smile warmed. "There's nothing wrong with a good fling now and again. I have them myself. But something tells me it would be more serious with you two, and I'd hate to see the summer end on a sour note. For any of us."

Corrine made a mental note to stop stereotyping people.

Greg's assistant producer had considerable smarts to go along with her other numerous skills.

Hopping off the stoop, Paulette called, "Ta-ta," to Greg and breezed past him. Luke had pulled his junker economy car to the curb to wait for her, and she climbed inside.

Without a word to Greg, Corrine returned to the kitchen and retrieved her backpack. He was still sitting at the picnic table when she set the security alarm and locked the door.

"No worries." She repeated her new personal mantra with each step that brought her closer to him.

Her determination faltered when he stood, grinned sexily and said, "Hi," with enough sensual firepower to remind her just what else he was capable of doing with that incredible mouth of his…and how much she'd like him to do it again.

"Come on. Let's walk."

"Greg…"

He fell into step beside her. "I'll be good. I promise." To demonstrate, he shoved his hands in his pockets. "My mother raised me to be a gentleman, and gentlemen don't let women walk alone in the dark."

"This woman's been trained in self-defense by the military. If anyone's in danger of falling victim to an attacker, it's you."

"Huh. Then maybe you should walk *me* home."

It was too dark to see her face but he sensed her guard slipping.

Good. Being nervous was an indicator of how much he affected her, and Greg liked affecting Ms. Uptight-Ex-Army. Last night he'd gotten a sample of just what lay on the other side of that barricade she was always erecting, and he wanted more.

He would, however, have to wait. Okay by him. Nothing worthwhile was ever easy.

Corrine was obviously on the same wavelength. "Where are Ben and Annie?"

"In bed. Sleeping soundly. I finally managed to wear them out today."

"You didn't leave them alone again?"

"Of course not. Russ is with them."

"That's good."

"Maybe not. He agreed to stay only because the twins are asleep. My patience wasn't the only one they tested today."

"What happened?"

"I brought Ben, Annie and Belle along on the shoot this morning. Let's just say it didn't go as planned."

"I could have told you that."

"I didn't have much choice. Briana wasn't available to babysit."

"She spent the day at an equestrian meet with her drill team."

"I was going to ask you for the number to the college, but you didn't make your usual rounds at lunch."

"I got busy."

"No problem. Alice put me in touch with Natalie, who gave me the name of her sitter. Hopefully, the lady will return my call tomorrow."

"What if she doesn't?"

Irene had asked the same question when she'd called that afternoon, at Russ's urging, no doubt, to read Greg the riot act.

"Tether the kids to a tree with a four-foot rope and plenty of water?"

"Don't even joke about that!" Corrine gasped.

Irene hadn't found it funny, either.

"Relax. I was thinking more along the lines of driving into

Payson and buying a thousand dollars' worth of toys to keep them busy."

"Or you could involve them in the shoot. They might be natural hams, just like their father."

"You have no idea how much I'd love to do that. Unfortunately, there are obstacles."

"What?"

"Russ, for one. He'd be a hard sell after the problems Ben and Annie caused today."

"Don't you get to decide who appears on the show?"

"Yes. To a degree. But it doesn't matter, anyway. Leah won't sign the release form. Without it, there's nothing I can do."

"Is she afraid the kids would get hurt?"

"I think she's afraid I'm going to corrupt them. Turn them into slackers like me."

"You're not a slacker."

"In her eyes I am. I'm going to talk to her when she comes out for a visit. See if I can't change her mind."

Greg and Corrine had rounded the dining hall and were passing a deserted stone fire pit, its embers still glowing from the after-dinner bonfire.

"You mind if we sit here for a while?" she asked.

"No." He concealed his delight, having assumed that, like last night, they were heading to her sister's cabin.

From their seats on the stone bench, they had a clear view of the main road, or would have had if it wasn't dark. Greg and the kids had trotted their horses down that same road on their afternoon ride. He'd nearly fallen off twice during the short sprint. Later on, while Ben and Annie frolicked in the shallow end of the pool, he'd soaked his battered body in the adjoining Jacuzzi.

"Do you ride?" he asked, wondering how much effort it would take to get the fire going again.

"I did when I was young. A lot more than I went fishing. Briana's our resident horseman. Make that horsewoman."

"How's this for an idea?" His hand itched to crawl across the stone bench and fold her fingers inside his. "I'll give you fishing lessons and you can give me riding lessons."

"Greg…" She exhaled slowly.

"That's sounding like a no."

"Even if I had the time, which I don't, it's just asking for trouble."

"What did Paulette say to you?"

"Nothing I haven't already considered myself."

"I'm going to fire her," he grumbled.

"No, you're not." She exhaled again.

"I know that me leaving after the tournament bothers you, but if things were to work out, we could still see each other."

"When your schedule allowed?"

"Well, yeah."

"I spent eight years in the army, remember? And saw hundreds of long-distance relationships. Some were successful, some weren't. Those that were successful required a tremendous amount of commitment."

"You think we wouldn't be committed?" He wondered if she'd been in a long-distance relationship that had failed.

"I think five weeks isn't a lot of time."

In the woods, an owl hooted. Much closer, crickets chirped and something slithered beneath a bush. Corrine paid little heed. Like him, she was completely at ease in the outdoors, even at night.

How could she think they weren't well suited to each other when Greg spent two-thirds of his life communing with Mother Nature?

"Is it Ben and Annie?" She was a little uptight around them. "Do you not like kids?"

"I like kids very much."

"How many do you want?"

"What does that have to do with anything?"

"I'm trying to get an understanding of all the obstacles I'm facing. Besides the distance—"

"It's not your job, it's mine."

So much for restarting the fire. Any illusions Greg had about a nice romantic evening faded.

"I don't have any issues with your job," he said.

"But I do." Though she studied the woods beyond the parking lot, her gaze had turned inward. "They called me 'the facilitator' in the army. I had a reputation, a well-deserved one, I might add, of getting things done and people to perform. It was a name I was proud of, one I strived to keep."

"You were good at what you did."

"No, I excelled. Whatever position they assigned me to, I outdid my predecessor. Whenever I was reassigned, I left shoes impossible to fill." Her voice lowered and cracked ever so slightly. "I can't figure it out. I put fourteen hours a day into *this* job—when I'm not fishing, that is—and I still can't get everything done. Can't motivate the staff. Can't pull off a single problem-free meal service. I'm so pathetic, I'm recruiting guests for dishwashers."

"We volunteered."

"Because I'm shorthanded and you feel sorry for me."

"Quit being so hard on yourself. The private sector doesn't operate like the military."

"I tell myself that every day. Jake every other day. It doesn't help. I was a soldier for eight years, and old habits are hard to break. Especially when I like the old habits."

"This is feeling a lot like a brush-off."

"Please understand."

Whether he did or didn't was irrelevant.

She rose, left him sitting at the fire pit, and walked the

remaining distance to her sister's cabin alone. Greg didn't have to be told he wouldn't be recruited to wash dishes tomorrow.

Or ever again.

Chapter Eight

Corrine was the last to arrive at the meeting. With an apologetic smile to everyone, she slipped into the empty chair beside Carolina. Their sister Rachel sat across the table from Corrine and next to their mother. Jake, his father, and his former brother-in-law, Aaron, rounded out the group of owners.

The only one not present was Corrine's other sister, Violet, who lived out of state. She'd sent their mother her proxy ahead of time, should any issues arise that required a vote. Corrine had sent similar proxies when she was in the army.

"Are we ready to start?" Jake asked. As head of the Tucker Family Trust, he presided over the meetings, though they all exercised their right to give input—frequently, and on occasion, loudly.

Not that they didn't love each other to pieces. The Tuckers might argue about how much money to allocate in the budget for cabin upgrades versus advertising, but they were thick as thieves, loyal to the core and unconditionally supportive.

They were also chatty.

"Okay, okay." Jake reminded them a total of three times before they quieted enough to start the meeting.

Corrine was the one exception. Other than hello, she hadn't uttered a peep from the moment she'd entered Founders Cabin, the place their monthly meetings were traditionally held.

As Jake read through the agenda, Corrine only half listened.

Her wandering thoughts landed not on work—where they usually were—or Greg—whom she'd seen only intermittently during the last two weeks—but on the cabin's original owners and the founders of Bear Creek Ranch, her grandparents, Walter and Ida Tucker.

From the mantel over the fieldstone fireplace, her grandmother's face smiled down at Corrine. The portrait had been taken in front of the present day dining hall shortly after it was constructed, in the early 1970s. Grandma Ida had been the ranch's first cook. She hadn't called herself a kitchen manager, probably because she'd run the entire meal operation single-handedly for the first decade that she and Grandpa Walter were in business.

Olivia may have been Corrine's first boss, but it was at her grandmother's knees that she had learned to cook for huge numbers of people and been inspired to uphold a Tucker family tradition.

If only her grandmother were here now to advise and assist her.

While Corrine had temporarily resolved her dishwasher dilemma—the student she'd hired would have to switch from full-time to part-time when the fall semester started—her problems continued to mount. The worst being morale. She'd been dreading this meeting all week, worrying that Jake would bring up her difficulties in front of the family. Not that they weren't already aware of them. Everyone on the ranch was, right down to the guy who came once a month to read the electrical meter.

What would Grandma Ida have done in Corrine's place?

Her gaze traveled the long conference table, from one person to the next. Those who noticed responded. Her mother winked at her. Her sister Rachel cut her eyes to Jake and then rolled them as if to say, *"Get Mr. Big Shot over there."* Her uncle's normally serious expression softened.

It occurred to Corrine that she would never find herself in a more loving, more supportive environment. These people truly understood her dilemma and wanted her to succeed. Not only that, they were counting on her. She was a fool to let pride stop her from seeking the help she needed.

"On to new business," Jake said. "Do you have those monthly occupancy reports?" he inquired of Alice, who sat beside him, taking notes on her laptop.

She immediately passed copies around the table.

"Wait!" At Corrine's outburst, everyone stopped what they were doing to look at her. "There's something I want to bring up that's not on the agenda."

For an instant, her courage failed her. Her mother's encouraging smile restored it.

"What's that?" Jake asked. He wore a similar smile.

"I'd like to discuss improvements I can make in the kitchen. And in myself as manager." Here was the hardest part, and Corrine faltered. "I'm open to your suggestions."

When no one broke into uncontrolled laughter or verbally attacked her, she let herself breathe again.

Jake commented first. "Then let's put our heads together and come up with a plan."

Any shame Corrine might have been feeling disappeared as her family came to her rescue, lending their experience, expertise and perspectives. When they were done thirty minutes later, she had in front of her a list of ideas that made sense and a heart full of love, hope and commitment.

She also had a renewed determination to be the best kitchen manager Bear Creek Ranch had seen since Grandma Ida.

THE REMAINDER OF THE meeting flew by in a blur for Corrine. Energized and excited, she couldn't wait to get back to the kitchen and begin putting into place the ideas she and her family had brainstormed. Her elation, however, plummeted when Jake brought up the last item on the agenda. Corrine chided herself for not listening to him earlier.

"How are Greg Pfitser and his family doing? I understand his film crew has completed shooting their first episode featuring the ranch." Jake turned to Alice, who consulted her notes.

"Yes," she answered. "His crew left yesterday. They'll be back at the end of July for another four days, and then again in mid-August for the tournament."

"Is there anything he needs from us in the meantime?"

"Not that he's mentioned. I understand he's planning on spending time with his children and working on his next book. He did inquire about attractions in Phoenix. I think they're planning to go down for a couple days."

"Good. How are reservations coming?"

"Up from last week."

"Any change in projections for the week of the tournament?"

"Still on target."

The collective sigh of relief was audible. So far, the plan to increase business was working. If all went well, their worries would be a thing of the past, for a while, anyway. If not…

Corrine's hopes that they'd gotten off the subject of Greg were dashed by Alice's next remark.

"The Pfitser children's mother, Leah Rusk, is scheduled to arrive next week. We originally booked her in the cabin next door to Mr. Pfitser's, but when I informed her of the arrangements, she requested one farther away."

"She sounds nice," Carolina said with fake sincerity.

"Actually, she was very cordial on the phone."

"Alice," Jake said. "I'm putting you personally in charge of her and the Pfitser children while she's here. I want them happy and entertained."

Corrine didn't contribute to the conversation. From what

Greg had told her about his ex-girlfriend, she imagined Leah either wished to distance herself from Greg, the children from him or both. Either way, it was no one's business.

Listening to others talk about him triggered a pang of misery. He'd evidently gotten the message and was steering clear of her. There were no more offers to help wash dishes, no more requests for tours, no more thinly disguised flirtations when she made her regular pass by his table at dinner.

There was no more kissing, either.

The lack of daily contact with him didn't stop her from remembering their indiscretion in vivid detail...or longing for it again. Neither did the silent lectures she delivered to herself on the average of three a day.

Corrine was torn, not a common predicament for her, and mad at herself. How could he have wormed his way past her defenses so quickly and so thoroughly?

More importantly, how could she get over him?

"Reservations are currently at ninety percent for the weekend of the fishing tournament," Alice informed the group, "and seventy percent for the weeks preceding and following. We expect those numbers to rise."

"How many people have registered for the tournament who aren't staying overnight?" Millie asked.

"About seventy. That number will also go up, but we're not sure by how much, as this is our first tournament."

Corrine started to mentally compile a list. Though these extra guests wouldn't be renting cabins, they'd be eating meals, three a day, as part of their admission cost. To pull off that kind of meal service without a hitch required tremendous and precise planning on her part. Hiring additional temporary staff for the event was the first order of business.

The tasks ahead didn't feel quite so daunting now that she had her family backing her. She might even involve Gerrie, give her assistant cook another chance to demonstrate her abilities.

Shortly after four-thirty, Jake adjourned the meeting. A few family members lingered to visit. Corrine wasn't one of them. She immediately headed outside to where her Jeep was parked. Founder's Cabin was located in a private section of the ranch, separated from the public sections by a good mile.

"Hey, can I catch a ride with you?" Carolina caught up to her on the porch steps.

"Sure. Where you going?"

"If I said to the Hitching Post for a beer would you join me?"

"No." Corrine laughed and checked her watch. "We start serving dinner in less than an hour."

"Drat." Carolina snapped her fingers. "How about the stables?"

"Since when do you ride?"

"Since a megagorgeous professional fisherman started taking his children on a trail ride almost every afternoon."

Corrine opened the driver's side door and climbed in behind the wheel. She didn't care for the gleam in her sister's eyes. Not that Corrine had even the tiniest claim on Greg, but still...

"I didn't realize you were interested in him."

"I'm not." Carolina dropped into the passenger seat beside Corrine and waggled her eyebrows. "You are."

"Am not."

"Are too."

They sounded like they were back in grade school. "Supposing I *was* interested in him."

"Which you are."

"There's no point in pursuing it."

Carolina snorted. "I beg to differ."

"Were you not just at that meeting? I have a huge amount

of work ahead of me in the next three weeks. We all do if we want this tournament to be a success."

"Don't tell me you can't squeeze an hour out of your schedule for a little social one-on-one."

Corrine remembered the last three disasters that had resulted when she squeezed an hour out of her schedule for Greg. Four, if she counted kissing in the kitchen.

"I'll take you to the main lodge or home," she said, attempting to end their discussion of Greg. "You pick." She started the Jeep and shifted into Drive.

"Spoilsport." Carolina sighed. "You are aware everybody knows that you and he like each other."

"What?" Corrine gaped at her sister, then turned back to the road before she lost control of the Jeep. Wind whipped in through the four open windows, blowing their hair around their faces. "Who's everybody?"

"The family. Mom figured it out and blabbed."

"Great." Not good, but not a disaster, either. Corrine could resolve the problem with some minor damage control.

"The employees, too. And not just the kitchen staff." Carolina smirked.

"What's for them to talk about? Nothing's happened between Greg and me." Nothing that anyone had seen. Or had they?

She rammed the vehicle into Third gear and took a bump in the road just a little too fast. They both popped out of their seats.

"The way I heard it," Carolina said over the noise, "is that one of the maintenance guys saw you and Greg cuddling up on his porch a couple weeks ago."

Corrine murmured an expletive. "We weren't cuddling."

"Hey, I'm all for it, remember? I'm the one who wants to go to the stable so you can 'accidentally coincidentally' run into him."

"It isn't going to work out between us."

"How do you know?"

"You were at the meeting. I can't afford any distractions. Not now. Besides, he's leaving soon. We both have our jobs to think about. And then there's his kids."

Corrine slowed down. "More important, there's the tournament and the cable TV shows and the business they'll bring the ranch."

"Yeah, yeah."

"You say that like I shouldn't care." Corrine swung the Jeep into the parking lot in front of the main lodge. Since Carolina hadn't indicated a preference, Corrine chose for her. A family with two older teenagers were checking in, their vehicle loaded with luggage and fishing equipment.

"I say it like someone who knows there's more to life than work and this ranch." Her sister abruptly straightened, reached over and grabbed Corrine's arm. "Don't make the same mistake I did. Don't let the love of your life go because of a misplaced sense of duty to a family who can survive without you."

Four years earlier, Carolina had been dumped by her fiancé because she'd chosen their family over going away with him. Not a day passed that she didn't regret her choice.

"I'm not in love with Greg," Corrine said softly, and placed a hand over her sister's. "We only met a few weeks ago."

"But you could be." Carolina's eyes misted. "Who's to say he's not the one? If you don't give yourself a chance, you'll wonder about it for the rest of your life."

Corrine tried to tell herself that her sister was being overly dramatic. But a niggling voice inside her started asking the same questions.

And the answers were unsettling.

"Can I help you, Mr. Pfitser?"

"I hope so."

After three full weeks at Bear Creek Ranch and literally dozens of visits to the front desk, Greg had stopped asking Natalie to call him by his first name. She stuck to formalities, as did every employee at the ranch with the exception of Corrine. She'd called him Greg, but not since the night she'd left him sitting at the fire pit. From then on, it had been "Mr. Pfitser" too.

Greg didn't like the change. There wasn't, however, anything he could or would do about it. Corrine had made her position on any potential relationship with him clear, and he respected her enough to abide by her decision. Considering he and the kids were leaving soon, it wasn't a bad one.

Given the opportunity, however, he might be inclined to try and persuade her differently.

"You haven't by chance seen a small black dog with floppy lips and bat ears running around?" he asked.

"Is Belle missing?" Natalie's previously helpful tone had become one of worry.

"For about the last hour."

"It could be worse."

They both knew that for a fact. Last week, Ben and Annie had slipped away at the stables and gone missing for a grueling forty-five minutes. After the place had been turned upside down, with all hands looking for them, one of the wranglers finally found them in a stall, playing with a horse and her young foal. Thank goodness the mare was gentle and not overly protective, or she could have gravely injured the children. Greg had given Ben and Annie a long talking to and made them promise not to wander off again without checking with him.

He obviously couldn't extract the same promise from Belle, and this morning, the dog had slipped under his radar.

"I'll call maintenance." Natalie had no sooner reached

for the phone than it rang. "Front desk." She glanced at Greg while she listened, then smiled. "Thanks, I'll tell him."

"Good news?" he asked when she hung up.

"That was the kitchen. They said to let you know they have your dog. They found her in the garbage and have her holed up in the restroom."

Greg grimaced. "I should have looked there first instead of the woods around the cabin."

"Well, the good news is she's been found and no harm done."

"We don't know that yet. There could be trash strewn from the kitchen to the parking lot."

"Give me a call if you need help."

"Thanks. Me and the kids will manage." He braced his palms on the counter and pushed off. "See you later today, I'm sure."

"Tell Corrine I said hi."

Greg stopped in midstep, not wanting to give away his excitement at that very prospect. "I will if I see her."

"Oh, you'll see her." Natalie's eyes gleamed mischievously.

Did she know something he didn't?

Ben and Annie were waiting on the lodge porch for him, enthralled with the yo-yos he'd recently purchased for them in town. Together they headed to the dining hall next door. Greg wasn't sure if the pleasure of seeing Corrine outweighed the reprimand he'd surely earned for letting his dog run loose and wreak havoc in the kitchen.

Everything at the ranch was meticulously maintained and neat as a pin. The rear of the dining hall was no exception. Every speck of trash was placed in a Dumpster hidden behind an enclosure built from logs that matched the dining hall. Beneath a ramada with a green shingled roof sat six weathered and battered picnic tables. A sign hanging from one of the posts said Employees Only.

Greg sat the kids at one of the tables, then made for the kitchen door. It opened a microsecond after he knocked. Belle shot outside and greeted him exuberantly, barking and trying to claw her way up his leg and into his arms.

She didn't get far. A sharp, "Sit, Belle," and a tug on the piece of twine that had been attached to her collar brought the dog to an immediate halt.

Belle plopped her round bottom on the ground, let her fat tongue loll and twisted her head to gaze adoringly up at the person on the other end of the twine.

"You shouldn't let her misbehave like that." Corrine had stepped through the door and stood on the short stoop. "She's not a bad dog. In fact, she'd quite smart. Just undisciplined."

Greg watched in amazement as Corrine led the dog toward one of the picnic tables. Belle heeled perfectly, like any graduate of dog training class.

"How'd you get her to do that?" Ben asked, abandoning his yo-yo.

"She already knew how."

"No fooling?" Greg went over to join them at the table.

"Haven't you ever asked her to heel before?"

"Um...no."

"Huh." Corrine gave him a look that would have been mildly insulting if he didn't deserve it. "Watch this."

She put Belle through a series of tricks that, besides sit and heel, included shake, lie down and roll over.

"Wow. I'm impressed." He was, as much with Corrine as the dog.

"Didn't the people you got her from tell you she was trained?"

He shook his head. "I don't remember."

"Here." Corrine passed him the twine. "You try."

"Me?" He balked.

"Go on. It's a leash, not a snake."

"Yeah, Daddy," Annie cheered, "it's not a snake."

"Fine." Greg took the leash. "I'm perfectly capable of being goaded into something I don't want to do."

Her second sigh was a satisfied one. After both of them stood there for several seconds like bumps on a log, she said, "Give her a command."

Since Belle was already sitting, he tried something different. "Stay."

"You have to walk away."

"I do?"

"First you tell her to stay, and then you step back. Haven't you ever owned a dog before?"

"No. My dad didn't like them, and I've been on the road pretty consistently since college."

"I'm surprised you remember to feed her."

"Belle's pretty good about letting the nearest human being know she's hungry."

"I bet." Corrine squared her shoulders, looking very much like the army officer she'd once been. "Now, repeat the command to stay and hold your hand up in front of you, palm facing out. Like this." She demonstrated. "Then step away."

Greg followed Corrine's instructions to the letter. Or thought he did. Belle responded by lunging at him and jumping up on his leg.

"Down, Belle." The dog ignored him. He repeated the command, only louder. If anything, Belle doubled her efforts.

"Ah-ah," Corrine said sharply, and clapped.

Belle instantly stopped clawing Greg's leg and swung her head around.

"Down."

Belle dropped to the ground, sat and resumed panting.

"How did you do that?" Greg was in awe. Belle had been an incorrigible tyrant from the day they'd brought her home, and yet Corrine had the dog wrapped around her little finger.

"It's not rocket science."

"What is it, then?"

"Dogs respect authority and respond accordingly. You don't have to be loud or mean or physical. Just firm." Corrine bent to pat the dog's head. "She wants to be good, and only misbehaves to get your attention. Now, try telling her to stay again. Only this time, be firm. And remember to reward her when she does what you want."

To Greg's delight, Belle stayed when he told her to and then waddled over when he said, "Come." Next, he told her to sit. She did, and he scratched her ears. "Good girl." Belle stared up at him with the same adoring expression she had with Corrine. "Unbelievable."

"See? Not hard at all."

"Can I try?" Annie asked.

"Me, too! Me, too!"

Greg handed the leash over to the kids, who busied themselves putting Belle through her paces.

"Thanks for not ripping into me when I got here," he said. "I deserved it for allowing Belle to sneak off again."

"You didn't do it on purpose."

"What's this? Is Corrine Sweetwater getting lax about rules and regulations?"

"Not at all, mister, so don't think you can get away with anything." The humor in her voice belied her stern expression.

Greg was captivated. He'd missed Corrine this past week, and the closeness they'd shared. As much as he wanted to wrap her in a warm hug, he resisted. Her barricades might be weakening but he doubted she was ready to tear them down.

"I'm thinking there's a lesson in all this for me."

"How so?" she asked.

"Authority, respect, obedience. Not that I should treat Ben and Annie like a dog, but some of the same methods might succeed with them. I don't have to yell at them to get them to listen and behave better."

"The man can be taught."

Corrine's warm smile almost brought Greg to his knees. She really was something else. What he wouldn't give for them to meet again in a different time and place, where they could continue what they'd started two weeks ago.

"Maybe the woman, too? You seem to have changed a little."

"I have, I guess."

"A full staff must have helped. I heard from Natalie you hired a new dishwasher."

"That, and other things."

His curiosity was piqued but he let her remark go. He was too busy thinking about what this recent softening in her demeanor could mean for him.

For *them*.

Chapter Nine

Corrine sat by herself at a picnic table in the outdoor dining area doing something she hadn't since the day she'd arrived at Bear Creek Ranch—taking a short lunch break. Voluntarily. And—here was the big shocker—not feeling guilty about it.

She took a bite of her turkey sandwich and contemplated the changes that had come about recently, starting with the family meeting when she'd spilled her guts. The next day, a new whiteboard was hung on the wall by the supply room, tracking deliveries for two weeks. Her idea. Yesterday, they'd begun cross-training employees from housekeeping and maintenance to cover in the kitchen. Her mother's idea. Lastly, they were about to implement an incentive program. Jake's idea. More changes were being considered, but for now, the ball was rolling in the right direction.

A squeaky creak accompanied the back door swinging open, and Gerrie stepped outside. In one hand she carried a plastic cup, in the other a sandwich. A hair over five feet tall and slightly pudgy, she frequently joked that she was built for strength, not speed. Kicking the door shut with her foot, she walked toward Corrine. "Mind if I join you?"

"Of course not." Corrine forced herself to sit still. Otherwise, she might have reeled back in surprise. Since the night the staff left early without cleaning, Gerrie spoke to her only about work, only when necessary and went to great lengths to avoid being alone with her. Corrine pretended not to notice—and not to be hurt by the intentional slight. "There's plenty of room."

Rather than sit at one of the other tables, Gerrie slipped onto the bench across from Corrine and immediately bit into her sandwich. "I'm starving today."

Corrine blinked. No, she wasn't imagining it. Gerrie was actually eating a meal—with *her*.

"I'm hungry, too, for some reason."

Actually, the reason wasn't a mystery. Kitchen workers ate at odd hours, before or after the guests were served. Depending on when their shift started, there could be long stretches between breakfast, lunch and dinner.

A moment passed, then Gerrie asked, "Have you hired extra help for the tournament yet?"

"No. I posted ads in a few places but I'm not having much luck." Because it was so unlike Gerrie to engage in casual conversation, Corrine couldn't help being suspicious. "I might have to break down and call a temporary labor service. I've been avoiding that because their rates are high and will blow my budget."

Gerrie took a sip of her soda. "You know I belong to Help for the Hungry."

"I've heard you mention it once or twice, though I'm not sure exactly what they do."

"Basically, we're an organization that provides meals to homeless individuals or families who've fallen on difficult times and aren't able to feed their children. Remember the flash flood we had last winter?"

"I wasn't here but Mom emailed me about it."

"Four families were literally washed out of their homes and left with nothing. The high school put them up in the gym for a few weeks until they were able to resettle, and Help for the Hungry made sure they had three squares a day."

"Wow."

"We also prepare a huge dinner every Sunday afternoon for the homeless or needy at the Grace Community Church. Anyone who shows up is welcome."

"That's really nice. And nice of you to participate."

"I was, um, talking to the administrator of Help for the Hungry, and we came up with this…sort of plan." Gerrie cleared her throat. "One that involves you and the ranch."

"Oh, okay."

Gerrie was probably going to ask the Tuckers to be a corporate sponsor. Or maybe seek permission for the organization to set up a table at the tournament. Corrine wasn't against it. Her family was active in the community and frequently sponsored outreach programs. But she would have to go to Jake with any request.

"He and I were thinking that Help for the Hungry could supply you with six or eight of our volunteer workers for the weekend of the tournament," Gerrie continued. "Enough to fill the temporary positions. And they'd work for free," she added hastily.

"Free?" Not what Corrine had expected.

"All right, not exactly free. They'd work in exchange for a donation to the organization, either monetary or food."

Corrine stared at Gerrie intently, her brow furrowed. "Are you serious?"

"Before you say no—"

"I think it's a fabulous idea!"

"You do?"

"Yes." Corrine placed both palms flat on the table. "It's perfect." She forgot entirely about eating her lunch and about her semi-feud with Gerrie. "I get the help I need, people who already know about food preparation and service and won't require much training. Your organization gets a donation. And the ranch can write off the donation on the income taxes. Everybody wins."

"Ah...yeah." Gerrie wore the expression of someone who didn't believe what she'd heard. She quickly recovered and broke into a wide grin. "So, you'll consider our plan?"

"Consider it? I'm going to run over to the office right now and talk to Jake. I'm sure he'll agree."

"Really?"

"Absolutely." Corrine stood, hopped over the bench seat and headed to the Dumpster, the same one the raccoon had raided the night she and Greg kissed, and disposed of her lunch remains. Her earlier hunger had been replaced by excitement. "I'll be back shortly."

"Wait a minute." Gerrie also stood, but with much less urgency. "Before you talk to Jake, there's something you should know."

"What's that?"

"I...um...that night a few weeks ago." She fidgeted, then blurted, "I'm the one responsible for leaving you to clean the kitchen alone. The staff had nothing to do with it."

"I see."

"I just wanted you to know how sorry I am. You didn't deserve that."

Corrine was speechless. Three times in the last ten minutes Gerrie had knocked her for a loop. Rather than feeling vindicated at having her suspicions confirmed, she felt only compassion for her assistant cook. Admitting wrong took courage as did apologizing. The least she could do was be gracious in return.

"Thanks for telling me." She nodded. "And I accept your apology."

"So, we're good?"

"Sure." Corrine smiled. "We're good."

"See you when you get back." Gerrie sat back down, her posture drooping with obvious relief.

Corrine could relate. "I won't be long."

"No need to rush. I've got everything handled."

For once Corrine had no doubts she'd return to a smoothly running kitchen.

She couldn't remember the last time she went to see Jake with good news to report. Confidence brought a spring to her step, a smile to her face and hope that the remaining pieces of her life would soon start falling together as well.

"HEY, THERE!" Carolina breezed into the kitchen as if she owned the place. "Let's go, little sis."

Corrine shot her a look. "Go where?"

"The Hitching Post."

She checked her watch. "It's seven-twenty. Even if I wanted to go out for a beer, which I don't, I can't leave for another hour. And besides," she added wearily, "I'm beat."

"Of course you're beat. You've been working seventy-hour weeks. Which is why you should leave now."

"I can't."

"Nonsense. You're the boss." Carolina's glance traveled the kitchen, encompassing the entire staff. Half of them were cleaning up from the dinner service, the other half prepping for breakfast the next morning. "You can manage without her the rest of the night, can't you?"

"Okay by me," Gerrie answered without the slightest trace of animosity. Jake's wholehearted acceptance of her idea to use Help for the Hungry volunteers during the fishing tournament probably had a lot to do with it, as did her and Corrine's newly mended fences. Amazing what a difference a single afternoon could make.

"Okay by me." Luke echoed Gerrie's sentiment, as did others.

"See?" Carolina lifted her hands in an oh-so-simple gesture. "The prisoners have freed the warden."

The dig to her management style didn't bother Corrine as much as it once would have.

"Go on, enjoy yourself." Gerrie shooed Corrine away. "You deserve a night out."

"I'd rather grab dinner someplace if you haven't eaten already." Bars and drinking had never been Corrine's thing. In the army, her visits to the officers' club were infrequent, usually to celebrate a birthday or promotion. "I'm not all that keen on the Hitching Post. Their food is pretty mediocre."

"Who cares? It's Thursday."

"What does the day of the week have to do with their food?"

"Thursdays are family karaoke night." Carolina's grin went from elfish to devilish. She came up behind Corrine and hurried her along by untying her apron.

Corrine dug her heels firmly into the floor. "No."

"Yes."

"My hair's a mess and my clothes are dirty."

"We'll stop by the cabin first." Carolina was clearly on a mission. "You can change and put on some makeup."

"You are not getting me up on any stage."

"We'll see."

"I sing awful."

"She's not that bad." Carolina looked over her shoulder and winked at the kitchen staff. "When we were kids, she used to sing in front of the mirror and record herself on her cassette tape player."

"I think everyone here could have done without hearing that childhood memory."

"Hey, I do that, too." A round of laughter followed Luke's admission. "What? Doesn't everybody?"

"Yes, they do," Carolina concurred. She'd maneuvered

Corrine to within a few feet of the door. "Which is why kar-aoke is so popular. Singing well isn't the point. Having fun is, and that's what we're going to do."

Corrine didn't know how her sister finally convinced her, but the next thing she knew, she'd changed clothes, put on some lipstick, and the two of them were cruising down the highway to Payson. The parking lot was packed when they arrived. Family karaoke night was obviously a popular and well-attended event. Some of Corrine's anxiety dimmed. With this many people vying for mic time, the chances that her sister would try and force her to sing lessened.

"We may not get a table," she hollered into Carolina's ear as they entered the honky-tonk.

The music was loud, the singer ten decimals louder and slightly off-key. The crowd, which included people of all ages, pressed shoulder to shoulder, didn't seem to mind, and ap-plauded enthusiastically when he finished. Corrine decided the place wasn't as bad as she'd anticipated. With so many parents and kids present, and just as many soft drinks being served as alcoholic beverages, it felt more like a neighborhood party than a local bar and grill.

"This way." Carolina grabbed Corrine's hand. "I have a friend here. He saved us seats at his table."

"What friend?" she asked, thinking it was someone from the Payson radio station, where her sister worked part-time.

"Over there!" She lead Corrine on a winding path among tables and chairs. Given the dim lighting, the multitude of patrons and Carolina's bright pink cowboy hat, Corrine could see no farther than a few inches in front of her nose.

In the next instant, they reached one of the booths along the far wall.

"Hi," Carolina said brightly, and with enough volume to be heard over the singer on stage. This one was belting out a halfway decent version of Keith Urban's latest hit. "Sorry we're late. Cinderella needed to get ready for the ball." She turned and gently pushed Corrine toward the table. "Well, what are you waiting for? Sit."

She couldn't move. Her feet had become cemented to the floor the second she saw her sister's "friend" and his two children.

"There's plenty of room." He scooted over, flashing his trademark lazy grin—the one that did funny things to her insides from the first moment they'd met.

A young preteen raced by, bumping into Corrine as he did and knocking her momentarily off balance.

"Hurry," Carolina urged. "Before we're trampled."

"Daddy's going to sing with me." Annie bounced in her seat. Her bright gaze fell on Corrine. "Will you?"

"I don't think so, sweetie."

"Of course she will," Carolina exclaimed. "Singing is the reason we're here."

Corrine highly doubted that. She recognized a setup when she saw one, and her sister had gone out of her way to set her up big time.

"Have you picked out a song yet?" Carolina asked Annie.

"Daddy said we had to wait for you."

"Well, come on." She helped the little girl out of the booth. "You mind?" she asked Greg.

"Be my guest."

Corrine snared her sister by the wrist before she escaped, pulled her close and whispered fiercely, "You're going to pay for this."

"*Au contraire,* my dear. I think one day you're going to thank me."

Not likely.

Carolina and Annie took two steps and were engulfed by the crowd.

With a great deal of reluctance, Corrine squeezed into the booth beside Greg. Across from her, Ben hunkered down until only his head showed above the table.

How she wished she could do the same.

FIVE MINUTES LATER, Carolina and Annie were back. Thanks to having five people in a booth designed to accommodate four, Greg and Corrine had to sit close. Closer even than the other morning on the boulder—which was just fine with him.

"Have you been here before?" he asked during a short break in the music.

"Once or twice when I was home on leave. Never for karaoke."

"What? No hidden pop diva or secret fantasy of fronting for a rock band?"

She shook her head. "Absolutely not."

"Are you telling me you never sing in the shower or while driving the car?"

Again she shook her head.

"She's such a liar," Carolina said with a laugh. She and Annie were comparing favorite artists over a beer and Shirley Temple, respectively. "Corrine sang so much that one Christmas Mom and Dad bought her a Mister Microphone."

"I'm going to kill you," Corrine said between clenched teeth. "And I have the skills to do it."

Carolina went on as if she hadn't spoken. "It worked with any radio. She'd shut herself in our room, turn on Mister Microphone and sing at the top of her lungs." Carolina pretended to plug her ears.

"Wow." Annie's eyes widened, and she practically salivated. "I'm asking Santa for one of those."

Greg decided if Leah didn't come through for Annie, he would. "Do you still have it?" he asked Corrine.

"Are you joking?" she answered fiercely.

He checked with her sister, who offered a noncommittal shrug. "I'll never tell."

"I heard you went to Phoenix for a few days," Corrine said.

"Daddy took us to the zoo and the movies and Castles and Coasters." Annie swung her legs excitedly, kicking the booth beneath them.

"Did you have fun, Ben?"

"I liked the Go Karts."

So had Greg.

"Sounds like you had a good time."

They'd done a lot, that was for sure. And definitely gotten to know each other better. But they'd yet to form the kind of close relationship Greg had been hoping for.

"How's the fishing coming?" Corrine asked.

"I'm still trying to convert the kids. They're learning, if not fully appreciating."

The music stopped, and the female singer on stage exited to a round of cheers.

"Nicely done, darling," drawled the DJ as he shuffled tiny slips of white papers. "Annie and her dad, you're up next." He scanned the audience. "What do you say, folks? Let's show 'em a little love."

The crowd applauded.

"That's us, Daddy." Annie literally crawled over her brother to escape the booth.

Ben clamped his hands to the sides of his head and groaned with feigned exasperation. His comical response was much more adult than Greg would have expected from a five-year-old and reminded him of his father in one of those rare moments when he'd allowed his human side to emerge.

"Daddy! Hurry." Annie stamped one foot, doing a fair imitation of her mother.

"Okay, okay. Give me a second." Greg's throat tightened and his heart swelled with pride. Ben and Annie were his children, and though he might not have been a part of their lives until recently, they'd miraculously inherited qualities from him and his family. It wasn't just his ego talking, either.

He smiled down at Corrine and waited.

She took the hint and slid out of the booth ahead of him. He made sure he stood right beside her and skimmed his fingers along her bare arm before allowing Annie to drag him to the stage and plunk a microphone in his hand.

He realized too late he should have gone with Annie to view the song books rather than let Carolina do it. Did Annie even know the words to Cindi Lauper's "Girls Just Want to Have Fun"? He didn't and relied on the teleprompter.

Greg didn't sing particularly well, but thanks to his livelihood, he was comfortable in front of an audience. Annie—big surprise—was a performance junkie like him. She knew enough of the lyrics to fake it. Laughter covered most of their blunders. His daughter was definitely a Pfitser through and through, and he enjoyed seeing her emerge from her shell.

He really needed to talk to Leah when she got here and convince her to sign the release forms so he could put the kids in front of the camera.

Near the end of the song, he took Annie's hand and twirled her like a ballerina. They were rewarded with cheers and whistles. When Greg stooped to retrieve her microphone, she flung her arms around his neck and kissed his cheek.

At that moment, he fell head over heels in love with his daughter.

"Oh, Daddy, can we do this again?"

He pressed a kiss to the top of her soft, wavy hair. "Every night if you like."

"That was fantastic," Carolina gushed when they squeezed back into the booth. "Annie, my sweet, you're a natural."

His little ballerina glowed.

Carolina went to work on Ben, but he seemed as determined as Corrine not to set foot on the stage.

"I'm surprised." She'd shifted slightly in his absence. "What you lack in talent you make up for in stage presence."

"I'll take that as a compliment." Greg missed the warmth generated from their bodies being in close contact. To correct the problem, he scooted over.

She noticed, of course, and scolded him. "You're incorrigible."

"I'll take that as a compliment, too."

He casually draped an arm across the back of the booth and, to his delight, her frown deepened.

"There are children present," she warned him.

"Let's sneak out back."

"Greg…!"

From across the table Carolina gave him a thumbs-up.

"I'm bored," his son complained. "Can I play pool?"

"I wanna play, too," Annie exclaimed. She and Carolina had put in a request for another song and were waiting to be called.

A mother, daughter and granddaughter took the stage and started singing "We Are Family" by Sister Sledge.

Greg wavered. Pool in a bar did seem a bit mature for soon-to-be-kindergarteners despite the proprietor's efforts to provide a family-friendly atmosphere by switching off the neon bar signs and turning up the lights. "Maybe when you're older."

"Other kids are playing."

Ben was right. Nonetheless, Greg hesitated. "I can't see the pool tables very well from here." He supposed he could go with them, but he rather enjoyed being the reason behind Corrine's obvious unease.

"I haven't played in ages. How 'bout I take them?" Carolina offered.

In a flash, Ben and Annie vacated the booth. Carolina was seconds behind them.

"Wait!" Corrine's loudly uttered protest went unheard.

Greg grinned.

"Forget it." She lifted her bottom and slid a good six inches away from him.

He took her rebellion in stride. "You're going to make this hard, aren't you?"

"Impossible."

"Why?"

"I told you. You're leaving after the tournament, and I'm not into long-distance relationships.

"Have dinner with me tomorrow night."

"What?"

"Briana's free to babysit."

"No."

"Come on. It's my last free evening for a while. Russ and Paulette will be here the day after tomorrow, and I'll be busy with them all week, getting ready for the tournament."

"I can't."

"I'll help wash dishes." Greg quickly calculated how much time he had left alone with Corrine before her sister returned with his kids. "I hear there's a pretty good country-and-western band here on weekends."

"I'm a worse dancer than I am a singer."

He let one hand dangle from the back of the booth to lightly caress her neck. "We'll dance only to the slow numbers."

She squirmed uncomfortably.

"What's wrong?"

"Damn, stupid tingles," she muttered.

"What tingles?"

She ignored his question. "I'm not going out with you."

"I'll pick you up at eight."

"I'm working."

"Wear jeans." He leaned in and nuzzled her temple. "Skin-tight ones if you have them."

"What makes you think I'm going with you *and* that I have anything in my closet besides camos and cargo pants?" She lifted her chin a notch.

Greg took it as an invitation. She resisted his kiss but not for long. Her lips, soft, warm and giving, molded to his, and for several seconds, he experienced heaven on earth—until they were rudely interrupted.

Not by the kids and Carolina returning, though that would have been awkward. No, this interloper was someone Greg hadn't expected to see until Saturday. Leah.

"Good God, Greg, have you no decency?"

Chapter Ten

Greg came up behind Corrine while she was checking the supply of breakfast condiments.

"I'm sorry about last night," he said. Fortunately for him, creamer was running low, giving him ten seconds to make his apology before she was free to run...or tear into him. The way he figured it, he deserved either or both treatments. "I had no idea Leah arrived early, much less tracked me and the kids to the Hitching Post."

"Don't worry." She turned around. "You couldn't help what happened."

"What? For a second there, I thought you weren't mad."

"I'm not."

"You should be."

She smiled.

So did Greg. "Does this mean you'll go out with me tonight?"

"No." Not only did her smile remain, she actually laughed.

"Can't blame a guy for trying."

She placed a hand on his arm. It was cool to the touch. Nonetheless, his blood warmed, as it had with each of their intimate contacts. She was so lovely, with her freshly washed hair falling around her face in soft waves. No one looking at her would have ever pegged her as a soldier.

"I want us to be friends, Greg."

"Wow." He drew back in mock surprise. "Don't we have to date awhile before I get the let's-be-friends speech?"

She lead him away from the condiment table and spoke quietly. "I don't think it's fair to either of us to start something we can't finish."

"Because I'm leaving in a few weeks?"

"And our jobs. Yours takes you all over the country. Mine is here. There's also your children. They need you now." Corrine angled her head in the direction of the entrance just as Ben and Annie burst into the dining hall, accompanied by their mother.

They'd gone home with her from the Hitching Post and stayed overnight in her cabin, stopping first at Greg's place to pick up their suitcases. After finding her precious babies in a bar, playing pool, and their father on the other side of the room putting the moves on Corrine, Leah had been livid. Greg half expected her to serve him with some kind of papers or a restraining order.

"Daddy!" Annie charged across the room, ignoring her mother's call to come back.

Greg admitted to feeling a small sense of satisfaction. It didn't last. Ben also made a move toward him, but Leah clamped a hand on his arm.

"I have to get back to the kitchen," Corrine said.

"We'll take this conversation up later."

"Greg, stop and think a minute."

"I am, trust me. You're all I can think about, day and night."

He spun around and scooped Annie up into his arms, giving her a huge hug. "Morning, cupcake."

"Bye." She waved over his shoulder.

He glanced behind him to see Corrine execute a hasty wave in return before disappearing through the kitchen door.

Annie squirmed to get down. "Hurry, I'm hungry."

Twice in one morning Greg mistrusted his hearing. "What did you say?"

"I'm hungry. I want pancakes."

"Well, I'm sure we can fix you up." He decided to risk life and limb and join Ben and his mother. If Greg was lucky, Leah would postpone her plans to give him a verbal lashing until they were alone.

"Hi, Daddy."

Greg liked hearing the easy way the words rolled off his son's tongue. Until they arrived at Bear Creek Ranch, both Ben and his sister had had trouble referring to him as their father.

Annie plunked down next to her mom. Greg occupied the chair beside Ben.

"Good morning, everyone."

"Morning." Leah's greeting was reserved but not quite as frigid as he was expecting, all things considered. "How are you?"

"Not bad." He appreciated that she was putting up a congenial front for the sake of the kids. Unlike last night. "About karaoke—"

"Don't worry," she said. "I'm not mad."

Okay, something was definitely wrong with his ears. "You're not?"

"I admit the idea of young children in a bar upset me at first."

That was an understatement. She'd hustled Ben and Annie outside, loaded them into the car and fled the parking lot, all in the blink of an eye. He still hadn't learned who at the ranch had told her where they were, not that it mattered. Leah possessed a built-in GPS system when it came to Ben and Annie.

Needless to say, the rest of the evening had gone downhill

from there. Greg, Corrine and Carolina left—in separate vehicles—as soon as the dust from Leah's exit settled.

"Once we got back to the cabin, the kids told me what a great time they'd had and how many other families were there." Leah squeezed a lemon wedge into her hot tea. "I might have jumped the gun a bit."

Before Greg could respond, one of the servers swooped down on them to take their orders.

"How's your cabin?" Greg decided not to press his luck, and changed to a neutral subject after the server left.

"It's rustic but quaint. The shower leaves something to be desired."

"Water pressure here in the mountains is hit-and-miss."

Their conversation, though cordial, bordered on awkward. It was to be expected, Greg supposed. Most parents in similar situations had spent years together before parting ways. They had a foundation of shared experiences and acquaintances to draw on, not to mention former feelings of love and caring. Greg and Leah didn't. She was as much a stranger to him as his own children were when he'd first met them.

"We have bunk beds." Ben spilled a few drops of orange juice in his excitement.

Their sleeping accommodations in Greg's cabin were twin beds and not nearly so much fun.

"Yeah." Annie pouted. "But I have to sleep on the bottom."

"Why don't you take turns? Let Annie sleep on the top tonight." Greg automatically wiped up the spilled orange juice with his napkin, beating Leah to the punch.

"I'm impressed." Her expression was actually friendly. "You're learning."

"What?" He looked at his damp napkin. "Oh, this." He chuckled. "It was either adapt or drown in the mess. I thought my film crew was sloppy. Ben and Annie put them to shame."

"Kids don't pay attention. Not at this age."

"Some adults don't, either, at any age."

She pursed her lips. "Is that an insinuation?"

"Yes. Directed at me."

"I see." She relaxed.

Ben and Annie weren't listening. They were busy building a miniature fort out of sugar packets, a bottle of Tabasco sauce and salt and pepper shakers.

"The last few weeks have been eye-opening for me. I've really come to appreciate how hard you've worked to raise these two single-handedly. And what a great job you've done."

"Thank you." She'd perked up. Her tone, however, remained reserved.

"Believe me, I don't want to take your place in Ben's and Annie's hearts. I think there's plenty of room for both of us."

She nodded solemnly. "They're all I have. It's been rough these last weeks without them."

"I bet." He was sure he'd relate when he returned them home to her in August.

"Mommy, Daddy. Look!"

Greg and Leah smiled down at their children's creation.

"Very nice," Leah said, her voice filled with maternal affection.

"Here." Using a toothpick and a torn corner from his paper napkin, Greg constructed a tiny flag. He gave it to Annie, who anchored it in the top of the tower.

"I want one, too."

Greg made a second flag for Ben, who stuck his in his teeth instead.

"He has your sense of humor," Leah commented.

"I don't know what you're talking about." Greg stuck a third flag in his own teeth.

Ben cracked up. So did Greg. He just might have found that elusive bond with his son he'd been searching for.

Their meal arrived. Ben and Annie attacked their pancakes like starving maniacs. Leah, on the other hand, toyed with her eggs.

"Is your food not good?" Greg's omelet was delicious, as were all his meals lately. Corrine's problems managing the kitchen seemed to be a thing of the past.

"Oh, no. They're fine." She smiled again. Weakly. "Annie's appetite has sure improved."

"Only today. You must be having a positive affect on her."

"I didn't—" she lowered her voice "—get pregnant on purpose."

"I never thought you did."

"Okay. I just didn't want you thinking I'd used you as a you-know-what donor. It was an accident."

"I'm glad it happened."

"Me, too." She pushed more food around on her plate. "I was sure the day you left with Ben and Annie was going to be unbearable."

"It wasn't?"

"No. And I think that upset me even more than them being gone. Don't get me wrong. I miss them. Terribly."

"Of course."

"But my world didn't collapse. And that was a shock."

Greg didn't quite know what to make of her confession. Given the five times she called every day, he'd assumed differently. He was debating on how to approach her signing the release forms when she dropped a bombshell.

"The extra time with Wayne is nice, too."

"Wayne?"

"He's a coworker." Leah's glance went quickly to the kids, who were demolishing the fort they'd built, in between bites of pancakes. *"And my boyfriend,"* she mouthed.

She had a boyfriend! Greg's knee almost hit the underside of the table. No reason to come unglued, he told himself. Leah was an attractive, successful woman and nice when not being a psycho mother grizzly bear.

"That's…good."

"Yes, it is." Her features softened. "We get along really well."

"Well enough to…?" He mimicked slipping a ring on his third finger.

"It's too early for that." Something in her voice indicated a marriage down the road wasn't entirely out of the question.

"I'm happy for you."

If this Wayne guy helped Leah to lessen her stranglehold on the kids so that she didn't go into a panic every time he took them away for a weekend or the summer, he was all for it.

"Ben and Annie like him, too."

"They do?" The egg in Greg's mouth turned to mush. "How much?"

"A lot. He's very good with them. But then he has a nine-year-old daughter who's just adorable."

Greg put down his fork. Suddenly this boyfriend thing had taken on a whole different importance.

He, Ben and Annie were just beginning to connect. Greg didn't like the idea of another man in the kids' lives. One who was there a lot more often than him. Perhaps even permanently. With an adorable daughter. They were sounding more and more like the perfect American blended family.

"Is something the matter?" Leah asked.

"No." He reached over and patted Ben's back. If Annie

were within reach, he'd have done the same with her. "Just getting full."

"The food here is really quite good." Leah appeared to have finally found her appetite.

"Corrine makes me the best macaroni and cheese." Annie abandoned the fort demolition project to join the grown-ups' conversation.

"Who's Corrine?" her mother asked.

"The kitchen manager," Greg stated, hoping Leah wouldn't make the connection.

"She had a Mister Microphone when she was a kid."

"What's that?"

"A microphone so you can sing songs on the radio." Annie pouted. "But she wouldn't sing with me last night."

Greg could almost see Leah fitting the puzzle pieces together.

"Ah." She arched her brows. "The woman at the bar."

"She's nice." Annie went on to list Corrine's many admirable qualities, ending with, "And she makes special food just for me."

"I'm glad you found a new friend." Leah's gaze traveled from Annie to Greg. "Both of you."

Greg stabbed at his omelet. He didn't like the turn their conversation had taken. How could he get mad at Leah for having a boyfriend when he'd be in the same shoes if Corrine would quit being so damn stubborn, and agree to go out with him?

"WHAT ARE YOU GOING to do?" Carolina asked.

"No clue." Corrine balanced an elbow on her sister's kitchen table and dropped her chin into her hand.

"Do you have any errands to run in town?"

"I suppose I could come up with something."

"Medical appointment to make? Paycheck to run to the bank? Dry cleaning to pick up?"

"Not really." Corrine was faced with her first real day off in three months. She'd managed to stay busy during the morning, helping with yard work, but mostly driving her sister crazy. The afternoon presented even less appealing possibilities.

"Old friend to look up?" Carolina carried the pitcher of fresh squeezed lemonade from the counter and refilled their glasses. While Corrine had finished pruning the rosebushes with military precision, her sister had fixed the two of them lunch. It was a nice change from eating in the dining hall.

"Except for you guys," Corrine mused aloud, "I haven't communicated with anyone around here in years."

"Why not?"

"No reason." She nibbled on a celery stick. "It just happens."

"Doesn't mean you can't pick up the phone and call. I bet most of your old friends would be happy to hear from you."

"I guess."

"You can't keep living in a cave, sis." Carolina returned the pitcher to the counter and sat down. Her kitchen was small and cozy and charming, having been furnished and decorated with purchases mostly from their mother's antique store, Trinkets and Treasures. "It's not good for you."

"If you keep nagging me, I might spend the rest of the day looking for different quarters."

"Good!"

Corrine knew her sister was only half-serious. Carolina liked the company as much as Corrine liked having a refuge on the ranch. She supposed she should be glad and grateful that things in the kitchen were running so well she could actually take time off. What she felt, however, was at loose ends and bored.

"How about your old army buddies?"

Corrine contemplated her sister's suggestion and agreed it wasn't a bad one. She could easily spend an hour or two on her laptop, reading and answering e-mails, a task long overdue. Hector's sister for sure. Corrine had promised to keep in contact with Rosa and had, more or less, until coming to the ranch. It was just so hard for her to sound uplifting and positive with Rosa, and harder still to read Rosa's e-mails detailing her and her family's struggles to go on without him.

"Hello! Sis, are you there?" Carolina snapped her fingers in front of Corrine's face.

"Sorry. I was just thinking."

"About that friend of yours who died?" Corrine had mentioned Hector to her, but not the depth of their involvement.

"His sister. You mentioned e-mails, and I remembered I owe her one."

"How's she doing?"

"Hanging in there, last I heard."

"How are *you* doing?"

"What do you mean?"

"Having a friend die is devastating. Especially so when you feel responsible."

Corrine almost gasped, but caught herself in time. "I never said I felt responsible."

"You didn't have to. I can read between the lines."

"There's nothing to read."

"Fine. If you say so. But I think you should talk to someone. A professional, maybe. It might do you good."

"Will you stop with the self-appointed therapist routine? I'm not messed up." Not much, unless she counted that mild case of obsessive-compulsive behavior.

"Take Greg Pfitser, for instance."

"Let's not talk about him, please." Corrine pushed back from the table.

Carolina ignored her. "The man has two things going for

him. One, he's gorgeous. Two, he's interested in you. *Very* interested." She gave an appreciative shiver. "You're a fool not to explore the many delightful possibilities with him."

"I remind you, he's leaving in two and a half weeks. Right after the tournament."

"Last I checked leaving wasn't the same as falling off the face of the earth. I'm sure airplanes will fly you and cars will drive you to wherever he is."

"I don't want a long-distance relationship."

"Why not? You sure as hell don't want a close one. I'd think a relationship with no strings attached would be right up your alley."

"There are always strings."

"So have an affair."

Hadn't Paulette given Corrine similar advise? "That's not my style."

"What is your style?"

Corrine didn't have an answer so ignored the question. "I don't want a boyfriend. I don't want an affair. I just want to spend the remainder of my first real day off doing something fun and relaxing and *solitary*." She emphasized the last word.

"Go rowing on Commodore Lake."

"Commodore Lake?"

She hadn't thought about her former haunt in ages. Situated about four miles south of the ranch, it was more like a large pond than a true lake. For a nominal fee, visitors could rent paddleboats by the hour. More tourists than locals frequented the lake, except for teenagers. Many a boat had been cut from its mooring and taken for a midnight excursion by adventurous, not to mention amorous, sixteen-year-olds.

"I'm not in high school anymore."

"You need to get away from this place." Carolina stood and

began collecting their lunch dishes. "I'd rather you connected with a living person, but if not, at least do something fun."

"Hanging out on Commodore Lake isn't fun."

"Okay. Have it your way. The steer manure and spreader are out back. I'll get th—"

"Maybe I will go." The idea of seeing Commodore Lake did strike a nostalgic chord in Corrine. "Just to see if the old place has changed any."

"Excellent!"

"I could bike there." The idea that had finally taken hold began to expand. The hills between the ranch and Commodore Lake were challenging but not grueling. She could do with a good workout. In the army, she'd pushed her physical limits on a regular basis. Here, she was lucky to fit in a few calisthenics after her morning run.

She began helping her sister clear the table.

Carolina shooed her away. "Go on. I've got this handled."

"But you cooked. Breakfast and lunch."

"And I'll clean," she said with a cheery smile. "You do it every day and need a break. I hardly ever get the chance."

"You could have had plenty of chances when I needed a dishwasher."

"Very funny."

Reluctantly, Corrine left the kitchen and headed to the spare bedroom she'd made her own. While she changed into bike shorts, her mind wandered. Her sister seemed ridiculously happy, almost as if she wanted Corrine out of the house for another reason. Was one of Carolina's many romantic interests on his way over? She'd gone cold turkey when Corrine moved in, toning down her semidecadent, frequent-cause-for-worry lifestyle.

Well, good. Carolina deserved a break, too. For that reason,

Corrine decided to stay away as long as possible. Perhaps until dinner.

To her surprise, her sister was nowhere to be found when she emerged from the bedroom. A note on the kitchen table offered a vague explanation about running over to the maintenance building and having one of the guys sharpen her gardening shears. Packing a couple bottles of cold water, Corrine went out behind the cabin and fetched her bike.

As she pedaled past the main lodge, she thought she caught a glimpse of Greg near the outdoor fire pit. He was talking to a woman who, from the back, looked a little like Carolina. On second glance, Corrine decided she must be mistaken. The maintenance building was on the other side of the ranch. Corrine continued to the highway, already feeling a slight burn in her calves and thighs.

Two hours later, she was seriously rethinking her plan.

The hills had grown into mountains during her lengthy absence, and the traffic had doubled. By some miracle, she made it to the lake in one piece before her legs completely gave out. The boat wasn't nearly as easy to navigate as she remembered, and almost impossible to propel. She felt as if she were paddling through quicksand instead of water.

"Forget it," she mumbled to herself, and attempted to steer toward shore without ramming into a pair of senior citizens having as much trouble as her, but enjoying themselves more. "This was a dumb idea."

Carolina would just have to kick her boyfriend out of the house, if one was even there. Corrine was going home. Better yet, if she hurried, she'd arrive at the kitchen in time to help the staff with dinner preparations.

Shielding her eyes, she took stock of her location. Exactly when had she paddled so far from the dock?

It wasn't until she was halfway across the lake that she realized it *was* her sister she'd seen at the fire pit and that her reason to get Corrine out of the house had nothing to do with meeting a man herself.

"Damn you, Carolina," Corrine said between heaving breaths.

Helpless, and with nowhere else to go, she continued paddling in the direction of the dock, watching as Greg, his children, his dog and—this was certainly awkward—his ex, tromped down the path to the shore.

Chapter Eleven

Greg was going to give Corrine's sister a huge kiss the next time he saw her. She'd obviously had a plan in mind when they'd "accidentally" run into each other after lunch and she'd insisted he take the kids to Commodore Lake.

What she probably hadn't counted on was Leah accompanying them. After their talk the other day, Greg understood Leah's overprotectiveness was just part of their joint parenthood situation. He decided he could afford to be patient with her for the remaining three days of her visit.

He might have insisted she stay at the ranch if he'd known Corrine would be at the lake—doing exactly what, he wasn't sure. He thought she might be trying to paddle in circles as fast as she could.

"Daddy, look who's here." For once, Annie was running ahead of Ben. Belle dashed after them, her leash trailing behind.

"Yes, I see."

"Annie, Ben, don't run!" Leah hurried after the kids and their dog.

Greg meandered, the only one not in a rush. The view was better higher on the lakeshore, and he rather liked seeing the normally competent, capable and athletic Corrine struggle with something so simple as paddling a boat.

"Hi, Corrine!" Annie stood at the end of the dock, waving excitedly. Belle was beside her, barking.

"Annie, get back here." Leah came up behind her and hauled her away from the edge. "It's not safe to stand so close to the water." She whirled on Greg. "You didn't tell me there were boats here."

"I didn't know."

While they talked, Ben attempted to climb into the nearest one.

"No! Ben, stop this instant." Leah was on the verge of having a meltdown.

She and Corrine both.

"Hey," Greg hollered. "You doing okay out there?"

"I'm fine." She had just narrowly avoided taking off a corner of the dock.

Annie escaped her mother's death grip and scrambled after Ben, who had one foot in the paddleboat and was working on a second.

"Greg!" Leah squeaked. "Do something."

"Ben, Annie, come over here. And bring Belle with you." His recently honed authority skills paid off, and the kids bounded over to him, dog in tow.

"See here." He pointed to a sign posted beside a large metal box. "All children under the age of twelve must wear a life vest and be accompanied by an adult while in the boats. That's you two. Here." He retrieved two bright orange vests. "Put these on and don't take them off unless your mother or I tell you it's okay."

"Can I go with Corrine in her boat?" Annie asked, fighting with the buckles.

Greg resisted the urge to help her. His independent daughter preferred to do things on her own. "I'm sure your mother would like you to go with her first." He'd seen the flash of disappointment in Leah's eyes. "Besides, I think Ms. Sweetwater's done for the day."

"Where's Belle's life vest?" Ben leaned over the box, his head buried inside it.

"She doesn't need one."

"But what if she falls in the water? She'll drown."

Belle was more likely to jump in the water. "Don't worry. All dogs can swim. It's instinctive."

"What's stink-tive?"

"It means born knowing how to do something."

Leah relaxed once the kids were properly secured in their life vests and drilled on water and paddleboat safety. Greg took out his wallet and inserted the required boat rental fee into a locked money box hanging from the signpost.

"Who's ready to take a ride?"

"We are, we are!"

"I want the blue one."

Greg helped Leah and the kids into a boat. She sat on one side of the rudder control, Ben and Annie on the other.

"Have fun."

He unhooked the rope, tossed it into the boat and gave the craft a push with his foot. They began drifting backward. Belle, stuck on the dock with Greg, strained against her leash.

"Sorry, girl. Didn't you read the sign? No dogs allowed on the boats."

"What about you, Daddy?" Annie might have popped out of her seat if not for her mother's restraining arm.

"There's not enough room!"

"I can't drive this thing alone," Leah complained.

"It's self-propelled. Like a bicycle. Pedal frontward to go forward and backward to reverse. Look at the other people."

"How does it steer?"

"The rudder. It's that handle beside you."

After a few false starts, Leah and the kids finally got the hang of it. Enough that Greg felt free to go over and check on Corrine. She'd finally managed to dock her boat and was crawling out of it on legs resembling cooked spaghetti.

"Need a hand?"

"No thanks, I've got it." She wound the last of the rope around the dock cleat and secured it tightly.

"Not with the boat."

"Sorry?" She tried to rise and instead collapsed onto her rump like a toddler taking her first few steps. An ecstatic Belle piled into her lap.

"Down, pup." Corrine gently nudged the dog away.

Greg reached out and lifted her in one easy movement. "Help with standing."

"Wait!" She wrapped an arm around his neck before her feet went out from under her again.

Her reaction was automatic, but that didn't stop Greg from taking advantage of the moment. "Steady, now." He wound his own arm snugly around her waist.

"I thought you and Russ were filming today."

"We were. This morning. He and Paulette are editing this afternoon and doing whatever other magic stuff they have up their sleeves. I only get in the way, so they told me to beat it." He brushed the pad of his thumb across her cheek. "You're face is pink. You forgot sunscreen."

"Damn, I did." She tried to wiggle free.

He held fast, telling himself it was for her own good. "Can you walk now?"

"Never again, I'm afraid."

She smelled great, like sunshine and cool breezes. His favorite scent. She felt even better, all weak and wobbly and womanly. A desirable change from her usual tough-as-nails self. And speaking of desire...

He hated letting her go, but did so before his body betrayed him. "Come on." He retrieved Belle's leash. "I'll help you up the hill to the parking lot."

"I can manage."

"Yeah? This I've got to see."

Corrine made it three steps before stopping to rest. "Stupid, stupid," she cursed herself, reluctantly accepting Greg's assistance.

He glanced backward. Leah and the kids were managing the boat fine and appeared to be having a wonderful time. If they even noticed him and Corrine, they gave no indication. He satisfied himself with knowing he'd have a clear view of the entire lake from the top of the rise and could reach the shore in a jiffy if they ran into trouble.

"Cut yourself some slack," he told Corrine. "Paddleboating is hard work. And you're out of shape."

"I am not out of shape!"

Damn straight. He's just been holding her next to him for the last few minutes and could attest to just what exquisite shape she was in.

Their progress up the hill was slow. They could have taken forever as far as Greg was concerned. He thoroughly enjoyed the climb, the beautiful view, the gorgeous weather and Corrine leaning heavily on him. Belle added to his contentment by being on her best behavior, walking obediently at his heels. He had Corrine and her sage advice to thank for that, too. She really was good for him.

Now, if only he could convince her of just how good he could be for her.

"Where's your car?" he asked when they reached the parking lot.

"I didn't bring it."

"How did you get here?"

"I rode my bike."

"You did what?" He drew to a halt and gaped at her. "Are you nuts?"

"That's it over there."

He should have figured out she'd biked, from ogling her skintight shorts and sports top. "No wonder your legs gave out. The ranch has got to be ten miles from here."

"Six point seven. I clocked it."

"Up and down the whole way."

"No lectures, please. I admit to being overambitious."

"I'm not lecturing. That's jealousy rearing its ugly head. I couldn't bike six point seven miles on a flat, straight road, much less these killer ones."

"Yes, you could. You're very fit."

He grinned. She'd been checking out his shape, too. "Why, thank you."

"It was an observation. Not a compliment." She braced a foot on the metal guardrail at the parking lot entrance and retied one athletic shoe.

"Sounded like one to me," he said, absorbed in studying her shape from this new and interesting angle.

"Take it however you want." Retying her shoe appeared to have sapped the last of her strength. Moving with the speed and agility of someone wearing a full body cast, she started out. "See you later."

"Where are you going?"

"Home."

"You're not riding that bike."

She stopped and turned. "That was my intention."

"You'll kill yourself."

"I'll be fine."

"You can hardly walk. Let me drive you home." He caught up with her in two easy strides. She wasn't going very fast, after all.

"There's not enough room in your SUV for me and the bike."

"There's plenty of room. The third-row seats fold down."

"The bike's too big."

"We'll take the front wheel off."

"You can do that?"

"You can't?"

"I'm sure I could if I tried," she answered with an offended huff.

"You could if you weren't ready to collapse."

"We need the right tools."

"Which I happen to have."

She planted her hands on her hips. Probably because holding them at her sides was too exhausting. "Don't you think the ride home will be a tad uncomfortable?"

He glanced down at the lake. Leah and the kids had completed one full circuit and were starting a second. From what he could see, she was letting Ben steer. Annie was tossing pieces of the bread they'd brought with them to the family of ducks following in the gentle wake of the small boat.

"Maybe," he agreed. "But it's a short drive, as opposed to a long and grueling bike ride. You don't want to wear yourself out so much you can't work tomorrow."

He could see his argument was having some effect. She must be a lot more exhausted that she let on.

Corrine in a weakened state did have a certain appeal.

Without warning, she threw a monkey wrench into his plans. "I'll call the ranch. Someone can come pick me up."

Luck was on his side. Her cell phone had no bars. Neither did his, which he proved by holding the phone out for her inspection. The only public phone in the area was one installed by the highway department to call for a tow truck in case of a vehicle emergency.

"Bikes don't count," he told her when he spotted her staring longingly at the phone. "Look, we're all adults here. Okay, not all of us," he corrected, before she could. "But Ben and Annie aren't the ones feeling uncomfortable."

"Okay," Corrine conceded. "Only if you can live up to your boasting and get the front wheel off the bike."

"I wasn't boasting."

She didn't acknowledge his remark. "Also, if Leah so much as crooks an eyebrow at me, I'm getting out and walking."

"Fine by me."

"Then we have a deal." She stuck out her hand.

He took it. In her depleted condition, a small tug was all it required to pull her off balance—and into his arms. He caught her and lowered his mouth to hers before she could object.

"I prefer to seal my deals another way."

"You're incorrigible," she said, and promptly melted against him, her arms going around his waist.

He kissed her swiftly but thoroughly, relishing the sweet taste of her and her even sweeter response. Their encounter ended too soon, leaving her breathless and flushed and him desperate for more. Unwilling to let her go, he set her slowly aside, letting his hands linger on her enticing curves.

"Rest assured," he said, more than a little breathless himself, "we're going to take this up later. When it's dark, and we're not standing in the middle of a public parking lot."

"You know I think that's a bad idea."

"Yeah, I noticed what a bad idea you thought it was, right before you hand snuck up my shirt."

"Not for one second was my hand anywhere near your shirt."

"Oh, yeah?" He pointed to his T-shirt, part of which had been tugged loose from the waistband of his jeans.

She looked mortified.

"Don't worry," he said, suppressing a smile. "We can take that up later, too."

"Not on your life."

Even she had to hear the complete lack of conviction in her voice.

"Come on. Quit your pouting and let's get the tire off that bike of yours."

Anger had rejuvenated her. She didn't require his help to traverse the short distance across the parking lot to the bike rack. She unlocked the chain and Greg wheeled the bicycle over to where the SUV was parked.

Within a matter of minutes, he had the front wheel off and the bike loaded into the cargo compartment, demonstrating that he was a man of his word.

Corrine didn't comment, but her eyes widened with appreciation—or was it gratitude?—when he returned the toolbox to its place under the rear seat and slammed the door.

"Mind if I check on the kids?"

"Not at all. Mind if I wait here?"

"I might be a few minutes." He tossed her his keys. "Get in and run the air-conditioning before you keel over."

She didn't have to be told twice.

"DADDY, DADDY!" Annie's and Ben's voices carried across the water to the dock.

"How're you guys doing?" Greg waved back.

"Ready to call it a day, I think," Leah said. She'd done most of the paddling, as Ben's and Annie's legs weren't quite long enough to reach the pedals. "At least as far as boating goes."

Greg caught the rope Ben tossed him and moored the craft. "You sure? We can wait awhile."

"Did Corrine leave?" Annie asked.

"Ms. Sweetwater," Greg corrected. "And no, she's going back with us."

"What about her car?" Leah's tone was difficult to interpret.

"She biked here and overextended herself. She can hardly walk, much less ride her bicycle back to the ranch."

"I see."

Small waves rocked the boat, which bumped into the dock. "Do you have a problem with that?" He helped Annie and then Ben out of the boat.

"Not at all. It's your vehicle."

He suspected Leah did have a problem, but wouldn't admit to it in front of the kids.

"Mommy, I don't want to go home yet." Annie held up her bag of bread. "I have to finish feeding the ducks."

"And you said I could catch some guppies." Ben had brought a small net and plastic Ziploc bag for just that purpose, which he extracted from his back pocket.

"What about Corrine?" Leah asked.

"She's okay for now."

"You sure?"

"Positive." Greg didn't confess that he'd disabled Corrine's bike so she couldn't get away even if she wanted to.

They spent another twenty minutes feeding ducks and catching guppies before Leah had a fit about the kids getting wet and muddy. Greg made a mental note to bring them back to the lake after she left, and let them muck around to their hearts' content.

Corrine was apparently dozing, and sat up with a start when Greg opened the passenger door to let the kids pile in. The discomfort she'd predicted came about when Leah realized Corrine would be riding in the backseat with the kids. Greg diffused the tension by suggesting she ride up front with him, an arrangement that suited him better, anyway.

He drove straight to Leah's cabin. He assumed she wanted

to be dropped off first, and the kids with her. As it turned out, he was correct.

"Bye, Daddy." Annie stood in the backseat and reached around the headrest to kiss his cheek.

"See you at dinner, sweetie."

He got a high five from Ben. "Be sure and put those guppies in a pail of water right away," he instructed.

Pulling back onto the road, Greg observed, "That wasn't so bad."

"Neither is a viral infection, but that doesn't mean I want one."

Belle stood with her squat front legs on the rear passenger window, staring after the kids and whining.

Greg headed toward Corrine's sister's cabin. "Don't sweat it. Leah will be gone on Sunday. You won't have to see her again after that."

Corrine hunkered down in her seat.

"She's nothing we need to worry about."

"There is no 'we.' "

"I was thinking the same thing in the parking lot earlier when your hand was inside my shirt."

She groaned. "Please don't bring that up again."

"I like it when you lose control around me."

"Well, I don't."

Here, in his opinion, was the crux of Corrine's dilemma, with him and with work. If she would just lighten up a little, unwind and let loose, she might enjoy herself more than she thought possible.

"Why is it so hard for you to trust other people?"

"I do trust people. Certain ones. Like my family and my commanding officers."

"Then is it yourself you don't trust?"

She twisted sideways in her seat. "If there's anyone in the world I trust implicitly, it's myself."

"Except around me."

Her mouth silently opened and shut, kind of like the nice rainbow trout he'd caught that morning. Then she turned away to glower out the window.

Carolina's cabin came into view.

"Great," Corrine grumbled.

"What's wrong?"

"My sister has company."

"Like in the kind of company you don't want to disturb?"

"I recognize the car." She laid her head back on the rest. "All I want is a hot shower, a couple of ibuprofens and a couch to lie on."

"I have all those things in my cabin."

"Forget it. Take me to the kitchen."

"You're not working tonight." He threw the SUV in reverse and turned it around. "If I have to kidnap you, I will."

"Don't be ridiculous."

"Let's go to my cabin. I promise not to make a pass."

She snorted.

"Scout's honor." He didn't wait for her to agree, and took the bend in the road leading away from the main lodge and dining hall.

She didn't make a fuss. Greg contemplated placing a hand on her forehead and checking to see if she had a fever to go along with her exhaustion. Corrine Sweetwater never went down without a fight. When they pulled into the parking space beside his cabin and she still hadn't murmured a word, he began to really worry.

She climbed gingerly out of the vehicle and followed him and Belle, her steps leaden. Still wondering what was going on with her, he inserted his key and opened the door. Belle scrambled inside. In the small space of time his back was turned, Corrine had walked over to one of the metal lawn chairs and plopped down in it.

"You're that tired?" He sat in the empty chair adjacent to hers.

"I'm that *scared*."

"Of what?"

"You." She pushed her sun visor back and gave him a rueful smile.

"Why? I promised to behave."

"And I believe you."

"So, what's the problem?"

She gazed up at him. "If I go into that cabin with you, what do you think the odds are we'll wind up in bed together?"

"Zero." He struggled to remain calm. It wasn't easy with his pulse suddenly skyrocketing.

"Be serious."

"Corrine." He took a risk and reached for her hand. "I repeat what I said in the car. I won't take advantage of you."

"What if I take advantage of *you*?"

"I can't lie. I'd be pretty darn happy if you did." He rubbed the back of her hand with his thumb, as much to relax himself as reassure her. "But that's not going happen. Not today." Unless he counted his imagination, which was busy putting him and Corrine together in a dozen different, intensely provocative scenarios. "You're too tired."

"Not that tired." She peeked at him through lowered eyelashes. "Especially if I was lying down."

Oh, brother.

Greg grabbed the armrest with his free hand. It was that or leap out of his chair and ravish her on the spot. To hell with his neighbors.

"Do you have any idea what you're saying?"

"Yes." Her answer drifted out in a whisper.

He wanted her, was beginning to think he'd go crazy if

he didn't have her—and soon. But she'd been the one to constantly put on the brakes, and he had to be sure of her commitment before they went one step further.

"You probably think I'm really stupid—Russ sure as heck would—but I feel compelled to remind you of the conversation we had a couple weeks ago. The one where you stated, adamantly, I might add, that you didn't want to get involved with me."

"I remember."

"What's changed your mind?" He sensed a return of the pressure he was applying to her fingers.

"I haven't changed my mind. Not in the way you think. You're still leaving soon, and I'm still worried about falling for you."

She was falling for him?

"Then why take any chances?"

"Because I've finally realized Carolina and Paulette are right."

"Paulette?"

Corrine nodded. "I've shut myself away for too long, scared of being hurt again. Scared of making mistakes."

No doubt about it. She was definitely squeezing his fingers. Somehow, Greg managed to hang on to the last vestiges of his control.

"Now you're not?"

"Hardly." She looked at him. "But I'm more scared of the regrets I'll have if we don't spend what little time you have left here together."

"What happened to you?" he asked tenderly.

"Can we talk about it inside?"

"Talking isn't what I'll be doing after we cross that threshold." He had a different method of communication in mind. One that involved a lot of touching and tasting and exploring all her soft, intimate places with his hands and mouth.

She stood, and for an agonizing second, he thought she'd changed her mind. He should have known she was made of stronger stuff.

Tugging on his hand, she pulled him to his feet, through the door and straight into the fantasy he'd been having about her since his first day at Bear Creek Ranch.

Chapter Twelve

"I want to take a shower first," Corrine murmured, her fingers trailing the line of his square jaw. He'd trapped her in a heated kiss the instant the door closed behind them, and had yet to let her escape.

"Can I join you?" He dipped his head to nuzzle her neck and the delicate skin behind her ear.

"No." Shivering slightly, she stepped back. Her hand remained on his cheek, cupping it, the pads of her fingers caressing the fine hairs at his temple. "I want you waiting for me when I get out. In bed. Naked." She sighed softly. "Because that's what I'll be."

Corrine wasn't being coy or seductive as much as shy. A day of yard work, biking and boating had left its mark on her, and she wasn't about to slide between the sheets with Greg without freshening up first. Reclining beside him in a darkened bedroom, entwining her limbs seductively with his, held far greater appeal for their first time together than a cramped shower. Though later on...

Well, he had mentioned more than once.

Leaving him standing near the front door, she turned and headed toward the bathroom. At the entrance to the hall, she stopped, struck by a thought.

"Do you have any protection?"

"Yes."

Good. The nearest convenience store was twenty minutes away.

Giving him a last glance over her shoulder, she slipped into the bathroom. Once inside, she leaned her back on the closed door and waited for the fluttering in her stomach to quiet.

Somewhere between sitting in the porch chair and walking inside, her exhaustion had fled. Adrenaline surging through one's body tended to have that effect. So did sexual need. Hot water cascading over her skin increased her awareness of that need, and by the time she was done showering, she craved Greg with an urgency she's never felt before.

When she exited the bathroom dressed in nothing more than a towel, she'd forgotten all about being shy, all about her earlier exhaustion, the difficulties of long-distance relationships, Greg's imminent departure in three weeks. She'd even forgotten about work.

There was only him, lying naked in the middle of the bed, a sheet pulled up to his waist, a strong, tanned arm propped beneath him and that damned lazy grin of his stretching from ear to ear.

She was going to have to do something about wiping it off his face once and for all.

It was easier than she thought. When she let go of the towel, it dropped to the floor and pooled around her feet. Greg's surprised expression was priceless, and Corrine almost laughed. Her sister Carolina would be so proud of her.

She approached the bed. He lifted the sheet and welcomed her in. She had only the briefest glimpses of his lean, muscular physique before he enveloped her in his arms and brought his mouth down on hers hard.

No worries.

Her new personal mantra drifted back to her through a haze of sensual delights and allowed her to let Greg take the lead. There would be plenty of opportunity to familiarize herself with every inch of him later. The rest of the afternoon and all through the long, warm summer night.

He abandoned their kiss to move lower, his lips burning a trail along her collarbone and to the valley between her breasts. Corrine arched her back and moaned. She was quickly learning the many benefits of going slow and easy. And who better to teach her than Greg Pfitser, the master of taking his time?

Her determination faltered when he first tortured and then soothed her aching nipples with lips, teeth and tongue. She barely managed to hang on when his equally skilled fingers parted her legs and delved inside her. All hope was lost when he moved lower still and replaced his fingers with his mouth. Lifting her hips, she threaded her hands into his hair and urged him to hurry.

As if Greg would ever do that.

"You are so going to pay for this," she said, her body taut, her nerves on fire, her every emotion focused on him and how exquisite he made her feel.

"Baby, this is only the beginning."

He was right.

And so was she.

After he brought her to a staggering climax, she turned the tables on him and played just as unfairly. Greg, it seemed, could dish it out a lot better than he could take it.

Draping herself across his middle, she took his erection in her hands and wrapped her fingers around it, then proceeded to make him wait. And wait. And wait.

"You're evil," he said, and grunted with frustration.

She blew a warm breath onto his lower belly. "Paybacks are hell."

Eventually, she put an end to his torment and took him into her mouth. He lasted a full ninety-three seconds before he hauled her onto his chest and anchored her to him with an arm resembling an iron vise.

"Enough of that."

"Are you sure?" She wiggled seductively, just to add to his misery. "What happened to the laid-back guy I know?"

"He left the room the second you walked in wearing only a towel." Without releasing her, he reached over and picked up the condom he'd left on the nightstand.

"You're going to need two hands for that," she cooed, and tried to slip away.

He tightened his hold. "Want to bet?" Using his teeth, he ripped open the package.

She watched in fascination as he removed the condom and sheathed himself one-handed. Good heavens. Was there no end to his talent? She couldn't wait to discover the answer and drew her legs under her in order to straddle his hips.

Greg braced his hands on her waist, positioned her above him and gently eased her down. Corrine gasped as he filled her, withdrew, and then thrust deeper and deeper. There was no going slow for either of them.

And no turning back.

The last rays of sunlight filtered in through the parted curtains. Watching the ecstasy of their joining play across Greg's face, she felt closer to him than she had to anyone. How could that be, when they'd known each other only a few weeks? Rather than question the impossible, she leaned over him, held his face between her hands and kissed him with a fervor that left her shaken and vulnerable.

His response was immediately and infinitely satisfying to both of them. Rising up off the mattress, he shuddered and clung to her so that she experienced the intensity of his release as much as he did. When it was over, he slumped back onto the bed, eyes closed and his breathing labored. She traced the contours of his face with delicate strokes until he calmed, marveling at how truly gorgeous he was.

Eventually, he opened his eyes and gazed at her with a tenderness she'd not seen in him before, but suspected had been there all along.

"You're incredible." There was that damn lazy grin again.

This time, she felt no need to eradicate it, and instead enjoyed being the one responsible for putting it there.

"You, too." Skimming her hands down his sweat-dampened chest, she said, "I can honestly say sex has never been that good for me."

He captured one of her hands and brought it to his mouth. Kissing the palm, he said, "I wasn't talking about the sex."

"No?"

"*You,* Corrine Sweetwater, are incredible. The sex was just okay."

She laughed and punched him playfully in the arm. "That is such a lie."

"You're right.' He rolled her off him and flopped onto his side so they were facing each other. "And if you give me a few minutes to recover, we can have another go at it."

"Maybe later."

"What?" His eyes widened.

She pushed away from him, swung her legs over the side of the bed and sat up. "I'm hungry."

"Now?"

"I've had an active day."

"And you're going to have an active night, too. So I guess some nourishment is in order."

"Do you have anything here to eat?" She didn't want to dress and go to the dining hall, where everyone would take one look at them and know what they'd been doing.

"A few things. For the kids, mostly. Toaster waffles, corn dogs, string cheese. Stuff like that."

"I cook for a living." She stood and then bent to retrieve her towel. "I can make a virtual banquet from almost anything."

He jumped out of bed. "I knew there was a reason I'm crazy about you."

"Are you?" She hadn't been expecting any declarations. This one touched her.

He stopped abruptly and pulled her to him. His gaze, intent and unwavering, caught hers and held. "Did you have any doubt?"

She laid a hand over his heart and felt it beating, strong and sure and, she liked to think, just for her. "Not at all," she whispered, and rested her head where her hand had been.

CORRINE SET A SECOND serving in front of Greg. For someone who'd claimed not to be hungry, he was certainly eating a lot.

"I have to admit, I've never had grilled peanut butter and jelly sandwiches before." He picked his up and examined it before taking a big bite. "They're pretty good."

Smiling to herself, she set the frying pan in the sink to cool. There was something intimate and rather indecent about eating a meal semidressed and with a man she'd just made love to. "My friend in the army showed me how to fix these."

"Hector?"

"You remembered." Corrine sat at the table beside Greg.

"Was he your boyfriend?"

She nodded, debating how much to say.

"You don't have to explain." Greg washed down his last bite with a large swallow of milk. "You're a beautiful woman. I'm sure you've had a ton of men after you."

"Not exactly," she scoffed, wishing she'd fixed herself another half sandwich so she'd have something to fiddle with besides her empty paper plate. "Hector worked under me. My prep cook."

"How long did you date?"

"A few months."

"Did you love him?"

"I cared about him. Given time, our feelings probably would have developed into love."

"Was he discharged?"

"He was killed."

Greg put his glass of milk down. "In combat?"

She swallowed. It was easier talking about Hector with Greg than anyone else, but still hard. "We didn't see a lot of action where we were stationed. Most of it took place in the next town over."

"An accident then?"

She paused, readied herself and took the plunge. "He was knifed to death. In cold blood. By one of the locals."

"I'm sorry, honey." Greg reached over and gathered her hand in his.

She gulped. "It was my fault."

"You were stationed in a militant third world country at war with its neighbors and, sometimes, with itself. How can anything like that be your fault?"

"Because I turned my back when I shouldn't have and failed to do my duty as an officer and a soldier."

"You saw him being murdered?"

"No! I couldn't live with myself if I had."

"Did you know beforehand that this local was going to kill him?"

"Of course not."

"Then his death couldn't possibly be your fault."

"You don't understand." The pain in her chest, the one

she'd lived with for months after Hector was killed, pressed against her lungs until she felt as if she couldn't breath.

"Are you all right?" Greg asked gently.

"Yeah." The concern in his voice steadied her.

"You don't have to talk about this if you don't want to."

"I do. I want to."

She *needed* to. And not with just anyone. Only Greg. He'd faced his share of personal demons when his father died, and carried a burden of guilt even to this day. Knowing he would understand gave her the courage she needed to face her own demons and, she hoped, conquer them. Forcing herself to breathe slowly, she continued.

"There was a family. A mother and six children. No dad. So poor you can't begin to imagine the horrendous conditions in which they lived. A homeless person over here sleeping on city streets has more than these kids did. And eats better. The mom was scarred and a partial invalid. Over half her body was burned when a car bomb exploded. The toddler she was carrying lost her foot."

"Oh, geeze."

"Sadly, their situation wasn't uncommon. The mother would send the two oldest kids to the base. They'd hang around outside the kitchen, begging for food."

"And you gave it to them."

"No, I didn't. Please don't think badly of me," she said, when she saw the look in his eyes. "Sneaking food to the locals was strictly prohibited and with good reason. We didn't know who was our friend and who was our enemy. Children included."

Encouraged by Greg's patient silence, she went on.

"I'm not sure how long Hector was sneaking food to those kids before I found out about it. I let him talk me into turning a blind eye. He was a goofball, nothing more than a big kid himself. He came from a family of twelve and didn't have much in the way of money or privileges growing up, though his family was rich compared to most in the town where we were stationed. He took a shine to these two kids, probably because they were about the same age as his youngest brothers."

"He sounds like a nice guy."

"He was a great guy. Heart of gold." Corrine blinked back the tears filling her eyes. "What I didn't know, what nobody in the kitchen knew, was that Hector had started taking the whole family food. He'd stuff his shirt and pockets with leftover rations, stow them in a box in the pantry and, don't ask me how, sneak the food off base and deliver it to that horrible little hovel they called home."

"He had to have help."

"No one ever came forward."

"Would you?"

"I did. I told my commanding officer everything I knew, and took full responsibility."

"What happened to you?"

Greg's hand had remained wrapped around hers the entire time. She took great comfort from that.

"I got my wrist slapped."

"That's all you deserved. You said yourself you had no idea he was taking food to the family."

"They killed him!" She choked back a sob.

"One of the children?"

"Their father."

"I thought you said he was gone."

"He came back. When Hector showed up with a box of food, the man stabbed him. He claimed he thought his family was under attack by the Americans, and that he acted in self-defense."

"Did the authorities believe him?"

She made a sound of disgust. "The authorities didn't care."

"What about the army?"

"There wasn't much they could do. Hector was in violation of strict regulations. He entered a local residence without the army's knowledge or consent."

"It doesn't seem fair."

"Hell, no, it's not fair!" Corrine's insides felt as raw as her voice sounded. "You know what's ironic? That man killed the one person responsible for keeping his family alive all those months he was gone."

"It was an accident. A terrible accident."

"Please. That was no accident. Hector was stabbed in the back at close range."

"Do you think if you'd known what he was doing you could have stopped him?"

"If I'd been a good soldier, reported him for sneaking food to the kids like I should have, not let my feelings for him cloud my judgment, he'd still be alive."

"You can't be sure of that," Greg said. "From what you've told me, he was a pretty determined and resourceful guy."

"I miss him."

"Of course you do."

Corrine started to cry. "He shouldn't have died over something so stupid as a box of rations."

The pain, sorrow and grief she'd bottled up for months and months broke free. Once the first tear slid down her cheek, there was no stopping them. Not until a hundred of them fell. Greg pressed a fresh napkin into her hand and she used it to wipe her eyes. Within seconds, it became a wet, crumpled mess.

"Shh, it's okay." He scooted his chair back and pulled her into his lap, cradling her as he had Annie that day by the pool, when her brother had pushed her in.

Eventually, Corrine spent the last of her emotions. Because being held by Greg felt so nice, she stayed in his lap, clinging to him. He didn't seem to mind and just kept stroking her back with those marvelous hands of his.

"Is Hector why you left the army?" he asked, when her trembling had ceased.

"One of the reasons. The main one," she amended. "I can't explain it, but something changed in me the day he died. Up until then I'd always been able to keep my perspective. Shield myself from the travesties of war. And trust me, I saw things that would give most people nightmares for the rest of their lives." She sniffed softly. "Now I can't, and I wish to God I could. If only to feel like myself again."

"What you went through and how you reacted are pretty normal and to be expected. You lost someone important to you."

"And a career I loved." She tucked her head into the crook of his neck. "You must think I'm really messed up."

He brushed her hair from her face and kissed her forehead. "I think you're someone who's suffered a terrible blow and is still dealing with it."

"Not very well sometimes."

"If you ask me, I'd say you're doing an amazing job."

She snuggled closer. "This helps."

"Does it?" he murmured into her hair. "Then you can avail yourself of my help anytime you want."

She slipped her hand into the waistband of his boxer briefs. "How about now?"

He stopped her before she went too far. "As much as I'd enjoy ravishing you on this tiny kitchen table, I won't take advantage of you in a weak moment."

"You're not." She bent her head and tugged on his earlobe with her teeth. "If anything, *I'm* taking advantage of *you.*"

He tensed and inhaled sharply.

Corrine smiled. She was getting to him.

"I want you to make love to me," she whispered softly. Seductively. "You promised me earlier that once wouldn't be enough."

"I did, didn't I?"

"I need you." She rubbed the arch of her foot along his shin.

"Is that all?" He brushed his lips across hers. "Just need?"

"No. Need hardly begins to describe what I feel."

She pressed her mouth fully to his, silencing them both. Even if she could put her feelings about Greg into words, she wasn't ready to discuss them. He'd affected her like no man before. Had gotten closer to her, physically and emotionally, than anyone had in years. Even Hector.

Corrine was well aware of how significant that was, but wasn't ready to acknowledge or explore it. Not yet. Maybe tomorrow, after she and Greg had spent the night together and become even closer.

Sweeping aside the paper plates, she hopped from Greg's lap onto the table.

He broke into his trademark grin. "I was joking when I made that ravishing remark."

She whipped her T-shirt over her head and flung it in the general direction of the counter. Wearing only her panties, she leaned back on her elbows, flashed him her naughtiest smile and said, "I wasn't."

Chapter Thirteen

"Good morning," Corrine called cheerfully as she entered the kitchen and hung her backpack on a hook by the door.

"Hey, how ya doing?" Pat was the only one to actually answer, and her enthusiasm left a lot to be desired.

"I'm great." Corrine grabbed a clean apron and looped the strap for the bib around her neck. She didn't let the mediocre reception bother her. She was walking on air these days. "Looks like we have a full house."

Workers were crammed two and three together at each station. Volunteers from Help for the Hungry were on board for training in preparation of the tournament this coming weekend. More would report this afternoon. They would rotate shifts for the next two days until their training was complete.

"You seem happy," Pat observed, moving sideways to make room for Corrine at the counter.

"I am."

Greg had a lot—make that *everything*—to do with her elation. Over the last week and a half, he'd done his best to entice her over to the dark side. They'd spent as much time together as their respective work schedules and his parenting responsibilities allowed. Between the babysitter he shared with Natalie, and Corrine delegating more and more of her duties to her staff, that came to a considerable amount. Then there were the mornings she skipped her regular run in favor of a leisurely breakfast with Greg, straggling into the ranch kitchen whenever she got around to it.

Like this morning.

Greg had been fishing one of the smaller tributaries of Bear Creek in preparation for the tournament. He hadn't taken the kids with him as he usually did. When Corrine had pulled up to the creek bank in the golf cart, blanket and picnic basket in hand, he promptly forgot about fishing, and they both forgot about breakfast—until later, when she happened to glance at her watch.

"You're late," Gerrie grumbled into her ear. "You were supposed to be here an hour ago." She had the decency not to reprimand Corrine out loud.

"I know. I'm sorry." She washed and dried her hands before picking up a knife to start slicing tomatoes. "It won't happen again."

"You said that yesterday."

Frowning, Corrine slammed the knife onto the cutting board with a tad too much force. It was as if their roles had been reversed, and she was the subordinate getting her butt chewed. Not a pleasant feeling.

She reacted by asserting her supervisory status. "How are the volunteers doing?"

"Good, so far. Our operation here is a little more complicated than they're used to, but they're hardworking and will catch on quickly. Plus they've worked together before, so that helps."

"Sounds like you have it handled."

"There's another problem."

"What?"

"The equipment rental company called. They miscalculated their inventory and don't have enough tables and chairs for us. I begged and pleaded and, when that had no effect, read them the riot act. Bottom line, there's nothing they can or will do."

"Okay." Corrine grabbed another tomato from the pile.

"That's it? You aren't mad?"

"You tried your best. They can't spontaneously manufacture tables and chairs and neither can you."

"What about the tournament? We have three hundred and fifty guests to feed. They'll need places to sit, and we only have enough room in the dining hall for two hundred."

"We'll figure something out."

"Well, we need to do it pretty quickly."

"Relax." Corrine patted Gerrie's shoulder. Her assistant cook really was too uptight. "What about the picnic tables in the employee dining area?"

"They're hideous."

"We'll cover them with linen tablecloths. Talk to housekeeping, see what they have."

"That still won't be enough." Gerrie's voice had begun to rise.

"We have three days to come up with a solution."

"What about Jake?"

"What about him?" Corrine didn't want to involve her cousin.

"He has a lot of connections in town, like the diner and the adult daycare center. Do they have tables and chairs we could borrow?"

Corrine hated admitting the idea was a good one. If her mind wasn't constantly cluttered with thoughts of Greg, she might have come up with it herself.

"I'll talk to him later today."

"All right." Gerrie bent even closer. "Are you okay?"

"I'm fine. Why?"

"You just seem different. Not your usual self."

"No. Everything's perfect."

"Sure?"

"Yeah." Corrine's wish to be left alone must have shown in her face, for her assistant returned to her station and training the volunteers.

Corrine could feel the stares of her staff burning into the back of her neck. Ignoring them was difficult, but she persevered, and eventually they lost interest and resumed their various tasks of cleaning up from breakfast and prepping for lunch.

After finishing with the tomatoes, Corrine escaped the kitchen and made her regular rounds in a half-empty dining room. Jake was there, sitting by himself at a table in the corner, nursing a coffee and reading some papers. He didn't appear happy. Had he found out she was late to work again? He motioned her over with a casual wave, but it felt more like a command to report.

"Sit down."

She stalled. "I'm making rounds."

"So, you'll miss them. It won't be the first time this week."

Yikes, that smarted. "Sorry." Corrine pulled out the chair across from him and slipped into it.

"I don't care that you're late. You put in enough hours the rest of the week, more than anyone else on your staff. What I do care about is the reason why."

She stiffened, her defenses on the rise, and exercised a diversion tactic. "Hey, the equipment rental company bailed on us. Can you pull some strings with your business associates in town and find us about ten folding tables and eighty chairs?"

"No problem."

"I need to check with housekeeping, too, and ensure we have plenty of tablecloths. Oh, we don't have enough stainless steel cutlery for the outdoor tables, either. I was thinking of purchasing some of that nice plasticware that's painted to look like steel. If they have any in town, that is. I meant to check the other day and didn't. Which reminds me, when is maintenance cutting the grass? We need to set up tables on the lawn."

Jake removed a small notebook and pen from the pocket of his shirt and placed them in front of her. "Here."

"What's are these for?"

"To take notes. That's quite a long to-do list you're reciting."

"Oh, I'll remember."

"You haven't so far. Most of those things should have been taken care of already. My guess is you forgot. Making lists helps."

"I've been busy lately."

"You've been preoccupied. With Greg."

"My personal life is none of your concern," she said tersely.

"I couldn't agree more. And as your cousin, I'm tickled pink you have a personal life. We were all beginning to worry that you were working too hard and not enjoying yourself enough."

"You and the family have been talking about me?"

"Of course. That's what we do. Talk about each other and stick our noses where they don't belong."

"So, unstick your nose."

"This is different. I'm not just your cousin, I'm the ranch manager and your boss. When an employee's personal life affects their job performance, I have a right and an obligation to stick my nose in as far as necessary."

How many similar talks had she had with her subordinates over the years? Sitting on the other side of the desk—or table, as was the case with her and Jake—was no fun, even if she did deserve the reprimand.

"If you're going to write me up, then do it and let me return to the kitchen." She pushed his notebook and pen back across the table and started to stand.

"Sit down." His gaze locked with hers and held fast.

Their standoff lasted for several seconds before she lowered herself back into her chair. "Anyone ever tell you that you'd make a formidable officer?"

Though he didn't smile exactly, the lines of tension around his eyes disappeared. "I'm not going to write you up."

"No?"

"But I am going to give you a warning. This tournament and the exposure we'll get from the *Fishing with Pfitser* show are important to us. If business doesn't pick up soon, more jobs could be at stake, including yours and mine. Before we struck a deal with Greg's production company, we'd laid off six employees. Luckily, we were able to hire four of them back. I'd have to lay them off again."

"I sit in on the family meetings. I understand."

"Good." He nodded. "Then you won't get mad when I tell you to separate work from your personal life."

She felt a pang deep in her chest. Being with Greg was wonderful. Nothing like she'd expected. She was also aware, at least in the back of her mind, that she was ignoring two very important things: preparations for the tournament and Greg's impending departure.

"The problem may resolve itself on its own."

"How so?" Jake asked.

"Greg and the kids are leaving next week."

"You're not going to see him again?"

"I am." Corrine attempted to soften the defensiveness in her tone. "We just haven't discussed the details."

"Whatever the outcome, I want you to be happy."

"Unless it interferes with my job."

"You do have a responsibility where this ranch is concerned."

"Is that what you told Carolina?"

"Your mother's the one blabbing to the family about you and Greg. Not me."

"I was referring to the past. When her relationships got in the way of her responsibilities to the ranch."

Jake straightened and pushed his coffee cup aside. "I liked Carolina's fiancé, and I supported her decision to marry him."

"I heard differently."

"Your parents were the ones who objected to the marriage. My one and only concern was that Carolina not lose her share in the family trust. If she'd married him, she would have had to leave the country for five years."

The terms of the family trust required that all members spend no less than eight weeks of every year at the ranch. Anyone who went a full two years without returning to the ranch would forfeit his or her share to the remaining seven owners.

"I left the country, too," Corrine murmured.

"As you well know, the trust allows for several exceptions, military service being one of them."

"She was in love with him."

"If it had been up to me, I would have gladly extended the two years to five. But I didn't establish the terms of the trust, our grandparents did."

"We could have taken a vote. Changed the terms of the trust."

"We did. I was outvoted."

"I...didn't know." What else had Corrine missed while she was away? Her burst of temper cooled. "I guess I should have asked you first before jumping to conclusions."

The realization that Jake had always been in their corner and not their parents' was disconcerting…and enlightening.

"If you decide to leave with Greg," Jake said, "I'm all for it, as long as you come home every year for the required eight weeks. If not, I'll hound you like I did Vi."

"Is being part owner of the ranch really that important?"

"Maybe not. But being a member of this family is."

"More than the love of your life?"

Jake's eyebrows shot up. "Is Greg the love of your life?"

Corrine felt herself flush. "No."

"Could he be?"

"It's too early to tell." She wasn't about to admit she'd been asking herself the same question each and every time she and Greg curled up in bed together.

Jake stood. "Maybe you and he should 'discuss those details' next week." He bent and kissed the top of Corrine's head, then left through the front entrance.

She didn't move. Instead, she sat in the middle of a nearly empty dining hall watching the staff bus tables, and counting the days until Greg's departure. There were nine of them, to be exact.

Not much time to decide the course of the rest of her life.

GREG HELD THE dining room door open for Russ, who waddled outside ahead of him.

"I think the food's gotten even better since my last visit." He patted his protruding stomach. "I don't even like Belgian waffles."

"You ate three of them."

"They were great." He groaned and adjusted the waistband of his jeans. "You weren't exactly eating light, either, pal."

"True." Greg had shamed himself by devouring two apple

cinnamon muffins on top of an omelet. "But unlike you, I'm not sorry."

"A man could get used to eating like this."

"I was thinking the same thing."

Russ's brow lifted inquisitively. "Spoken like someone thinking of settling down."

"Why not? I have two kids who need a place to stay when they visit me, which is going to be often. Where better than here? They'll have plenty room to run and explore, build tree houses, ride horses and maybe even learn to fish."

Greg had been debating moving his home base from Wyoming to Denver to be closer to the kids. The last few days, those thoughts had turned to the ranch. Voicing them aloud made them sound all the better.

"It's kind of strange hearing you talk about settling down," Russ said. "You've been on the road, what, six years?"

"Closer to eight."

There was only one glitch to his plan that Greg could see. Corrine might not be ready to have him take up residence in her backyard.

Russ paused at the path leading to the parking lot and Greg's SUV. "Where are you giving casting lessons?" He held up a map of the ranch on which Greg had scribbled notes about the tournament, then turned it sideways. "I don't see anything marked."

"I haven't decided yet."

Russ lowered the map. "What's stopping you?

Greg thought fast. He should have anticipated the question and prepared a response. No, he should have already selected a location and noted it on the map.

"There are several decent meadows within walking distance from the lodge. I thought we could go together and look at them."

"Together?" Russ glared at him. "Please tell me you're joking."

"That way you can personally check the lighting and angles."

"I assume the meadow's outdoors?"

"Is that a trick question?"

"Yeah, to see if your head's screwed on straight. I don't give a flying fig which meadow you use so long as the lighting's natural, as in sunlight. And angles?" He snorted. "I'll shoot from the top of a tree if I have to."

"You're right. I should have picked the site out ahead of time."

"Damn tootin'. Along with the beginner pools." He jabbed the map with his index finger. "I see intermediate and advanced, but no beginner, and only three streams. You expect two hundred people to fish a handful of pools and three streams?"

"I was going to make another run this morning before you got here."

"What happened? We weren't early."

No, Greg had been late.

He'd taken advantage of his children's tendency to sleep in, and had cuddled with Corrine on the couch. She'd kept trying to talk to him, but he would have none of it. Next thing he knew, Russ had called to say they were almost to the ranch. Corrine left after that. Okay, not right away. They'd lingered at the door until she'd reminded him of her conversation with Jake the day before, and her commitment to be less tardy.

"The tournament starts in two days, and you're nowhere near ready." Russ shoved the fingers of his free hand into his thinning hair and groaned. "This isn't like you, buddy. What's wrong?"

"Nothing."

Everything. Greg been in a fog all week. When Corrine wasn't occupying his time, she was occupying his thoughts. Mostly, he was devising ways to get her out of the kitchen and alone with him. His lack of preparedness was the price he'd paid, though he didn't regret one moment with her.

"Is it the kids?"

"They're fine. A little cranky since Leah left." And nothing Greg did seemed to improve the situation. Their constant bickering and squabbling was getting on his nerves. He did his best to remain calm. The three of them had taken too many steps forward in their relationship to move backward now.

"Leah giving you grief again?" Russ's tone had changed to one of compassion.

"No. If anything, she's better. We were able to clear the air on a few things when she was here."

"It's the other one, then." Russ tapped his temple as if to jump-start his brain. "Corrine. The kitchen manager."

Greg swallowed. Was he that easy to read?

"You and she got a thing going?"

"We're seeing each other."

Russ tilted his head and studied him critically. "You've fallen for her, haven't you?"

"Yes," he said, finally acknowledging the full extent of his feelings for Corrine to someone besides himself.

"Well, I'm glad. You deserve some happiness." Russ abruptly grabbed Greg's sleeve, bunching the fabric between his fingers. "Now, if you don't mind, I'm going to kick your ass across whatever meadow it is we pick out *together.*"

"Hey!"

"Your timing stinks. Couldn't you have waited until after the tournament to take up with her?"

"I'm leaving after the tournament."

Russ let go of Greg's sleeve. "All the more reason not to do anything stupid."

Being with Corrine was the least stupid thing he'd ever done.

Their conversation was cut short by Russ's van pulling into the parking lot. Paulette sat behind the wheel. With her were Ben and Annie. Greg had a sinking feeling in the pit of his stomach. Paulette had driven the kids back to the cabin after breakfast to wait for their babysitter to arrive, which was only supposed to be a few minutes.

"What's going on here?" Russ grumbled.

"Let's find out before you get mad."

They crossed the lawn to the parking lot. The kids scrambled out of the van and came charging toward Greg. Belle ran alongside, nipping at their heels.

"Daddy, Daddy!"

"Where's Cindi Lee?" he asked, ruffling Ben's hair and patting Annie's cheek.

Paulette joined them. "She's sick."

"What?"

"Strep throat."

"Why didn't she call?"

"Apparently, she did. All morning. You're not picking up."

Greg removed his cell phone from his belt and flipped it open. *Dead.* He'd forgotten to charge it last night.

"That girl, Natalie, at the front desk. She has all the details. Your nanny called her, and she called me when she couldn't raise you."

"What are you going to do?" Russ demanded.

"I don't know." Greg had been counting on Cindi Lee's help during the tournament. "Talk to Alice, I guess."

"What about that teenager?"

"Briana? I can ask." Greg didn't hold out much hope for

her availability. All the Tuckers were working their buns off during the tournament, and that included Jake's daughters. "I heard she was manning the information booth."

"Damn it, Greg. You've got to get it together. We're running out of time."

"Lower your voice." He pulled the kids close and shot Russ a warning look.

"I wouldn't have to lower my voice if you had a babysitter."

"It's not my fault she quit."

"But the rest of this mess is." Russ started pacing angrily. "Maybe you don't care about a regular paycheck, but Paulette and I do. If *Fishing with Pfitser* tanks, so do we. You know this business. One day you're the number one show on the cable network, and the next you're canceled. I like being part of number one."

Greg couldn't argue. He'd let Russ and Paulette down. Worse, they weren't the only ones. He'd also let the Tuckers and their employees down. They'd worked hard and were counting on the tournament to boost their business. And they'd been hosting him, his crew, the kids and Leah over the summer at no cost.

"Don't worry. I'll have everything handled by the end of the day."

"Like you've handled it so far? Damn it, Greg."

"Enough!"

Greg glanced down at Ben's and Annie's small faces, which were pinched with worry and fear. He doubted they understood what Russ was saying, but they'd clearly picked up on his fury. Greg took hold of their hands and gave them a reassuring smile.

"I have an idea," he said to the group.

"What?" Russ had stopped pacing.

Paulette, who'd been standing to the side during her co-worker's tirade, showed interest.

"We put the kids in front of the camera. With me. I've been wanting to all along, but Leah refused to sign the release."

Russ stared, his expression deadpan. "You've lost your freakin' mind."

Paulette had the opposite reaction. "It's a fabulous idea."

"Absolutely not!"

"Our ratings will soar."

Russ glowered at her, then turned to Greg. "No offense, but your two rug rats aren't exactly obedient."

"Kids, why don't you take Belle with you and play over there." Greg pointed to the horseshoe pit.

"We want to go swimming."

"In a little while."

"What about horseback riding?"

"This afternoon. Daddy's kind of busy right now."

"You are not using me and Paulette to solve your babysitting problem," Russ said the moment the kids were out of hearing.

"So what if he is?" Paulette countered. "It's still a great idea."

"Give it a shot," Greg said. "What have we got to lose?"

"A camera, to start with," Russ answered. "Remember that day on the bridge?"

"I won't bring the dog. That should help."

They discussed the pros and cons of using the kids in various scenes. Russ was beginning to show signs of weakening when a pair of guests approached. They'd obviously just come from registering for the tournament, and carried canvas bags with the show's logo printed on them.

"Mr. Pfitser?"

"Yes." Greg put forth his best smile. It took some effort.

"We watch your show ever week." The first man extended his hand.

Greg shook it as well as the other man's. "Thanks. Nice to meet you."

"Me and Rusty here are from Albuquerque." He nudged his fishing buddy. "We came here just to see you, didn't we, Rusty?"

"Yes, sir, Mr. Pfitser."

"Call me Greg."

Rusty reached into his canvas bag and withdrew a T-shirt with a picture of the ranch on the front and Fishing with Pfitser on the back. "Mind if we get your autograph?"

"Not at all." Greg tried not to fidget. He really wanted to continue talking with his crew, but meeting these two men had reminded him of another responsibility. This one to his fans. He signed the T-shirts with a marker Paulette handed him.

"Thanks, Greg." Both men beamed.

"Good luck Saturday." He shook their hands again.

Paulette had used the interlude to work on Russ some more, speaking to him in whispers while Greg chatted with the men. Her powers of persuasion were nothing short of miraculous. Maybe he should include her in his phone call to Leah, Greg mused.

"Fine." Russ relented at last. "We'll try it your way. *If* Leah signs the release."

"I'm thinking of offering to bring the kids back a day or two early, or flying her out here so she can watch the filming."

"Better get to it." Russ sent a look to Paulette. "You have a script to revise." Then he hitched a thumb at the kids. "And they have one to learn."

Greg sprinted to the porch to collect Ben and Annie. After he called their mother and secured her agreement—by begging, pleading or throwing himself at her mercy if he had to—he'd take them with him to pick out a meadow and beginner pool.

Maybe Corrine could go with them.

No, wait. Scratch that, appealing though it was.

If he was going to redeem himself, make his idea of putting the kids in front of the camera succeed, he'd have to be all business and no play for the next four days.

Corrine would simply have to understand.

Chapter Fourteen

Corrine stifled a yawn. Four hours sleep last night and five the night before wasn't cutting it. Neither was the quart of black coffee she'd drunk this morning. She glanced at her watch and moaned. Four forty-five in the morning. She and her staff had opened the kitchen at a record breaking three-thirty. Shortly after that, the volunteer helpers arrived. No wonder Corrine wasn't the only one looking sleep deprived.

She considered the very long, very grueling day ahead of them and hoped they had the strength and stamina to survive it.

The tournament officially got under way at dawn. In order for participants to be able to eat before heading to their assigned spots, the dining hall had started serving breakfast two hours early. They would continue service until eight, as usual, to accommodate other guests. For lunch, tournament participants had a choice. They could either return to the dining hall or, if they preferred to continue fishing, pick up a box lunch from one of three stations throughout the ranch.

Dinner promised to be just as arduous, but for different reasons. Propane grills had been set up behind the kitchen. In exchange for a small donation to Help for the Hungry, participants could have their catch cooked up fresh and to order. The idea, Corrine's, was a great one. Not, however, easy to execute. And if the guys in Maintenance didn't locate two more propane tanks, her great idea wouldn't get off the ground.

"Come on, people, let's hustle." Gerrie's command, intended for someone else, served to rattle Corrine loose from her mental meanderings.

She picked up her pace, something she'd been doing since her meeting with Jake. Unfortunately, the problems had continued to stockpile, at a rate faster than she could resolve them. She felt as if she was back to square one. Worse than square one, because this time she had no excuse.

What had gone wrong?

Rhetorical question. She knew the answer. It was Greg and the enormous amount of time she'd spent with him. Without a strong leader, the kitchen had fallen apart. Again. Corrine had failed her staff, and unless she pulled a rabbit out of a hat, she'd fail her family, too.

She'd planned to talk with Greg about cooling it until after the tournament, but she hadn't seen hide nor hair of him for two days. She should be relieved. Without him to distract her, she could concentrate on her job. Only she wasn't. Instead, she worried.

Had his feelings for her changed?

No, not possible. There had to be another, logical reason for his sudden absence.

She'd heard from Natalie that he was every bit as busy as she was. On top of that, he'd lost his babysitter. Corrine assured herself that come Sunday evening, they'd pick up right where they left off…for approximately three days.

After that, he was leaving to take the kids back to their mother in Denver.

What then?

One of the servers burst into the kitchen. "We're out of orange juice."

"We can't be," Corrine exclaimed. "There were seven containers only yesterday."

"One container," Pat corrected. "The rest were grapefruit."

"Why didn't you say something?"

"I did."

"Not to me."

"To you," she insisted, her irritation apparent.

Corrine bit her tongue. Bickering wouldn't help matters. "Gerrie, get on the phone and call the supplier."

"I will, but what do you bet the soonest they can deliver is tomorrow afternoon?"

"What else do we have in stock besides grapefruit juice?"

"Apple and tomato."

One of the Help for the Hungry volunteers returned from the dining hall. "We're running low on sugar and creamer. And half a dozen people complained about the bacon."

"What's wrong with the bacon?"

"Burned."

"Let's make more."

"If we do," Gerrie said, "we won't have enough for tomorrow."

"I don't care." Corrine buttered toasted bread at the speed of light. "Do it."

"You sure?"

"Send one of the volunteers into town for supplies. Conduct a quick inventory first and make a list."

"That'll leave us shorthanded."

"It's either that or run out of food."

"There are no clean dinner plates left," one of the cooks complained. "We've got ten orders to fill and more coming in."

Corrine looked over at the dishwasher. It had just started

the spray cycle. "You two." She pointed to a pair of volunteers assembling box lunches. "Start washing dishes by hand."

Gerrie barked out quick instructions to the volunteers, then left her station to start on the inventory.

Corrine immediately stepped in and took her place. Working as fast as she could, she slit open packages of bacon and laid the strips on a broiler pan.

"Hey!" Gerrie's voice carried from the pantry door. "You two can't be in here."

Corrine turned to see who'd come into the kitchen. For one insane second, she hoped it was someone she could put to work. No such luck.

Ben and Annie stood at the end of the hall.

"Where's your dad?" she asked.

"He's outside teaching people how to fish," the boy answered.

There was a bright side, Corrine supposed. At least the kids hadn't brought the dog. Keeping one eye on them and the other on the counter, she continued to peel apart strips of bacon and arrange them in the pan.

"Who's watching you?"

"No one." Ben inched farther into the kitchen, Annie glued to his side. "Cindi Lee's sick."

"Does your dad know you're here?"

He lifted his shoulders in an exaggerated shrug.

Great. The kids were wandering the ranch unsupervised again. Corrine didn't automatically blame Greg. Ben and Annie likely took off whenever his back was turned, and with the tournament getting under way, his back was being turned a lot.

"Corrine..." Gerrie's tone held a less than subtle warning.

"Look, guys, you can't play in here. We're really busy."

Annie peeked around Ben. "Please can we stay? We won't touch anything."

Corrine wouldn't bet on that.

"Sorry." Her patience was running out. "Gerrie, call the front desk and tell Natalie to locate Greg. He's probably yanking his hair out right about now." Balancing the broiler pan in one hand, Corrine opened the oven door with the other. A blast of heat struck her in the face, and she averted her head. "Whoa, that's hot."

"I can help." Ben ran forward and reached for a dial on the oven.

"Don't touch that," Corrine snapped. "You'll hurt yourself."

He jumped back and collided with one of the volunteers. The stack of clean plates she'd just washed slipped from her hands and crashed to the floor, shattering into a thousand pieces. The volunteer yelped. So did Ben. Annie covered her ears and started to cry.

"Oh, my gosh!" The horrified volunteer stood with her hand over her mouth.

"It's okay," Corrine said. "We'll get it cleaned up. Just start washing more dishes."

The woman returned to the sink, still in a daze.

"We need plates," the cook called. "I can't hold these orders forever."

"One minute, hang tight." Corrine pushed the volunteer along. At the sound of crunching china, she spun.

Ben and Annie were stomping through the pile of broken shards.

"Stop where you are." She quickly slid the boiler pan of bacon into the oven. In her haste, she touched the red-hot rack with her bare fingers. The pain was instantaneous and excruciating. She jerked away, automatically balling her hand into a fist. "Get out of the kitchen this minute!"

Cringing, Ben and Annie backed away.

Had she yelled? So what if she did? The situation called for it, having rapidly gone from troublesome to dangerous.

Gerrie came up beside her. "Are you all right?"

"I'm fine."

"Natalie's putting the call out for Greg."

"Good." Corrine glanced at the kids. Confused and upset, they continued to spread china shards across the floor and get in the way of the volunteer trying to sweep up. "Have someone wait with them outside at one of the tables."

"You can't tell us what to do." Ben's defiance, dormant for the last few weeks, resurfaced with a vengeance.

"News flash, young man, I can." Corrine didn't think, she just spoke. "This is my kitchen and my ranch. The safety of everyone here is my responsibility. That includes the guests, the employees and you two." She pointed at each of them. "One of these nice people here is going to take you outside, where you'll park it until your father arrives. Do you under-stand me?"

Annie's features crumbled.

Ben's turned to granite. "We don't need anybody to take us."

"I think you do." Corrine didn't trust them. They'd gotten away from their father more than once. "Come on." She reached for his shoulder. If she got Ben to go with her, Annie would surely follow.

He wrenched out of her grasp and swore at her. His word of choice was very adult and not what Corrine would have expected to hear from a five-year-old's mouth. Taking advan-tage of her surprise, he broke free and ran from the kitchen. Annie wavered for only a moment, then hightailed it after him.

Corrine muttered her own expletive and started toward the door. Luke, fortunately, was seven steps ahead of her.

"I've got them," he said, and escorted the kids outside. They were too surprised to object.

Corrine tried to calm herself.

Gerrie approached once more. "Go bandage your fingers."

The first aid kit was kept in the restroom. After cleansing and bandaging her burns, Corrine returned to her station. The mess from the broken dishes had been removed and disposed of, the bacon was done cooking and the staff was back to operating like a well oiled machine. If she could just keep it together for the next couple of hours, she'd have a small window of opportunity midmorning to move whatever mountains she could.

The phone rang and the closest person grabbed it. "That was Natalie. She just wanted us to know that Pfitser one is on his way now to retrieve Pfitsers two and three."

Corrine could have sworn she heard the entire kitchen sigh collectively.

A few minutes later, she gave a quick glance out the window, just to make sure all was well. Greg was at that moment approaching the picnic tables. Catching sight of him, the kids escaped Luke's trusty watch and bolted forward. Their father grabbed them in a giant hug bear hug.

Satisfied, Corrine returned to work. She was more than a little surprised when he suddenly appeared in the kitchen.

"Do you have a second?" he asked.

She wiped her damp hands on a towel. "Only a second. We're really busy." She'd missed him the last two days, and if not for the other fifteen people in the immediate vicinity, she would have shown him how much.

"Can we talk outside?"

"I really can't leave right now." Noting his furrowed brow, she asked, "What's wrong?"

"I'm a little concerned about what happened."

"Don't worry," she assured him. "No permanent damage done. We got the mess cleaned up and are back on track."

"I am sorry they caused a problem. I don't know what possessed them to come here." He lowered his voice. "But I was referring to your treatment of the kids."

Corrine's voice rose slightly. "My treatment of them?"

"Annie's inconsolable. She's crying so bad I can hardly understand a word she's saying. Ben told me you yelled at them."

She was stupefied. "Yes, I yelled. Can you blame me?"

"You know how I feel about that."

"Ben was tampering with the controls on the oven. They broke dishes. Caused me to burn myself." She held up her bandaged hand. "I did what was necessary to defuse the situation."

"I didn't realize. Are you all right?"

"I'll live." She gritted her teeth to prevent herself from blurting what was really on her mind—that Greg had assumed his children were blameless.

He looked around the kitchen. "Are you sure you can't go outside?"

"I'm sure." She'd already spent too much time away from her station as it was. The rhythm the workers had reestablished was quickly deteriorating.

"I'd really like to talk about this later."

"Okay," Corrine agreed, though she didn't see why he was so upset. Maybe once he had a couple hours to calm down, he'd see the situation differently.

Greg left through the back door. Corrine returned to work, the unsettled feeling in her stomach refusing to abate. She tackled one chore after another, unable to afford expending mental energy on anything other than cooking.

The crew managed to survive the remainder of the breakfast service with only one or two minor mishaps. By ten o'clock, a hundred fifty box lunches were packed and ready to be loaded onto the pickup truck. Every dish, cup, fork and glass had been washed and stacked in preparation for lunch. The floor was freshly swept and mopped. Some of the staff were even taking a short break and enjoying a quick bite.

Corrine focused on breathing deeply. If not for her staff's stellar performance and exemplary teamwork, they wouldn't have come through half so well.

"Thank you, everyone," she said loudly, so they could all hear. "Good job! I wish I could say it's downhill from here but I'd be lying."

"We'll be fine." Gerrie nodded approvingly. "You did pretty good yourself."

"I don't deserve any credit. I let you all down these past couple of weeks."

"No, you didn't."

Corrine shook her head. "Come on. I was chronically late to work, shirked my duties, blew off my responsibilities and forgot half the things people told me."

"Hmm." Gerrie pursed her lips thoughtfully. "And here I thought you were delegating responsibility and giving us a chance to fly solo."

"You did more than fly solo. You pulled my fanny out of the fire."

"I don't know. I'd say it's the other way around."

Corrine couldn't talk past the lump in her throat. This was the kind of relationship with her staff she'd been hoping for when she started as kitchen manager. Funny that it took a near disaster to pull them together. Granted, they still had challenges to face over the rest of the weekend, but Corrine was confident they'd sail through them.

"I couldn't have done it without you," she said softly.

Gerrie grinned. "If you're any nicer to me, I'm going to ask for a raise."

"I was thinking more along the lines of a commendation."

"What?" Gerrie scowled. "This ain't the army."

No, it wasn't. But this small kitchen and these few individuals might be something Corrine could learn to love just as much.

She pushed off the counter. "What do you say we grab a sandwich and talk more about that raise."

"Really?" Gerrie glowed.

They got as far as the hallway, where they were stopped by Greg coming in through the back door.

"HI." CORRINE WAS GLAD to see him despite what had transpired earlier.

"You free now?" he asked.

Apparently a couple hours passing hadn't calmed him down any. His brown eyes regarded her without the usual warmth that sent tingles up her spine, and his mouth was set in a firm, flat line. The previous knot in her stomach returned.

"Sure."

He held the back door open for her. She squeezed past him and headed outside. Their bodies brushed ever so slightly, but the rush coursing through her was one of doubt and concern, not pleasure.

"I know you're upset that I yelled at Ben and Annie," Corrine said the second they were alone. The ranch was teeming with visitors and activity, the sounds of which floated to them from every direction. She and Greg, however, were relatively secluded behind the dining hall, and unless someone accidentally stumbled upon them, they could carry on their conversation in privacy. "But they were running amok and not listening to what I said."

"They're only five."

"Five's old enough to comprehend simple instructions, like 'you can't be here' or 'leave now.' "

"But not old enough to understand the complex operations of a commercial kitchen."

"I don't get why you're upset with me. I didn't do anything except try to protect your children from possible danger."

"I can absolutely see that, and I appreciate what you did. But you weren't with those kids afterward. They were pretty distraught. They're not used to adults…"

"Demanding they behave, for their own good and the good of others?"

"You know I don't approve of negative reinforcement."

"Ordering them out of the kitchen after they've caused an accident isn't negative reinforcement. It's averting a potential disaster."

"I agree. It's just—"

"You don't like my methods."

"When I looked at their faces afterward, all I could see was myself at their age. I don't want them to grow up like I did."

"You think I'm a bully like your father?" The thought horrified Corrine.

"Of course not. But your first instinct is to yell."

"Did it occur to you that Ben and Annie wouldn't have been in the kitchen in the first place if you'd kept a better eye on them?" There. She'd said it.

Greg clamped a hand to the back of his neck. "I realize you think I'm a soft touch, but I love them." He let his hand drop. "I hate to admit this, but I didn't before we came here. I wanted to, knew I should, figured I was a lousy father because I didn't feel a connection with them from the very beginning. By some miracle, it happened over the last few weeks." His voice thickened with emotion. "These two great little human beings are my kids. I couldn't be prouder of them or love them more if I'd been at the hospital the day they were born."

"I'm glad for you. That's the whole reason you came here and agreed to sponsor the tournament."

"It is. What I didn't expect was to meet you."

His words might have been a declaration of affection had his expression not resembled her commanding officer's on the day he'd told her Hector had died. Corrine's mild anxiety escalated. This was no minor difference of opinion they were having.

"What's wrong?" she asked him.

"You were right what you said about the kids being the most important thing in my life right now. I've been forgetting that these last few weeks. Until this morning." His cell phone rang again. He checked the caller ID before disconnecting. "You and I don't just have different approaches to disciplining children. We're two very different people, with vastly different approaches to life."

"Which could make us a good team."

"Or drive us apart."

"If we let it. Which is what you're doing."

"I'm being realistic."

"And you've decided, on your own, that the odds are stacked against us."

"You've said as much yourself."

Greg's cell phone rang yet again. This time, he answered it. "Yeah, Russ. I'll be right there. Give me one more minute," he said after a pause. His eyes cut to Corrine.

She resisted the urged to flee and hide. While she completely accepted that his children were important to him, she was profoundly disappointed with his easy dismissal of what they'd found together.

"Ben and Annie are going to be a permanent part of my life

from now on." He appeared to be collecting his thoughts. "I'm going to buy a house in Denver so I can be closer to them."

Corrine didn't need a map to know where that left her. "You're breaking up with me."

"Believe me, I never wanted to hurt you."

But he had. And everything she'd been afraid of was happening.

Tears filled her eyes and clouded her vision. She figured she had two choices: either let Greg witness her falling apart, or her staff. She chose the latter and stumbled up the stoop to the kitchen door.

"Corrine, please."

She stopped, her hand on the doorknob.

"I'm sorry."

"Have a safe trip back to Denver."

"Will I see you before I leave?"

"Only when I make rounds."

Once inside, she went straight to the restroom and stayed there for ten minutes, crying into a scratchy paper towel and willing her staff not to come check on her.

Balancing her job and her relationship with Greg was no longer a dilemma. He'd solved it for her. Even through her misery, she could see he wasn't totally wrong. They *were* different people. But given a chance, those differences could have been what kept their relationship spontaneous and interesting through the years.

Washing her face in the sink and adjusting her ball cap, she prepared to return to work. There were still problems to handle, a dinner to serve and tasks to accomplish. Always before, her strong sense of duty and strict adherence to regimen had carried her through the rough patches.

It had also given her an emotional shelter behind which to retreat.

This time, however, wasn't the same.

This time, she'd fallen in love.

Chapter Fifteen

Greg couldn't recall when he'd had a worse day.

For starters, he'd spent the better part of last night pounding his pillow rather than sleeping. Secondly, Paulette was on a roll and riding his ass hard, complaining nonstop about one thing or another that wasn't done or hadn't been handled correctly. This afternoon, she reached fever pitch when Greg forgot about and completely missed an interview with a Phoenix-based television station. Lastly, his two not so precious offspring were squabbling and picking on each other to the extent that Greg had left the room more than once in order to keep from blowing his stack.

He didn't require years of parenting to understand the reason behind their behavior. They were sensing his stress and responding to it, and, boy, was he stressed in spades.

Catching glimpses of Corrine off and on since yesterday morning didn't help his mood. While he believed he wasn't wrong—not entirely, anyway—he regretted his shabby handling of their disagreement. In hindsight, he should have waited until after the tournament. Then they wouldn't be quite so miserable, but more able to do their jobs. Though, from what he'd observed, Corrine was faring considerably better than him. Maybe because her staff was behaving and not pushing one another down, pulling each other's hair and calling each other names every chance they had.

"Ben and Annie, pay attention."

"Four, three, two, one, action," Russ called.

Greg knelt between his children. They each held a pole, at the end of which dangled a small trout. "Well, what have you got here, guys? Tell me a little about the fish you caught."

"We didn't catch these fish," Annie said, her rosebud mouth pursed in concentration. "That man over there did. He gave them to us, and you told us to hold them."

"Cut," Russ hollered. He removed the camera from his shoulder. "Greg, pal, did you not work with these kids?"

"I did." He had, last evening, and this morning at breakfast. "The concept of a script might be over their heads."

"We're on a very tight schedule. The awards ceremony is less than an hour away."

Greg was well aware of their time constraints.

Participants were gathering in growing numbers in the parking lot, weighing and registering their catches for the day. There were a dozen different prizes up for grabs. The grand prize winner, in addition to receiving cash and brand-new fishing equipment, would be featured in an episode of *Fishing with Pfitser*. With so much at stake, most participants had fished right up until the last possible moment, creating a severe bottleneck at the judges stand.

Russ had decided the controlled chaos would make for a great backdrop. And he would have been right if Ben and Annie cooperated, even a little. Greg still believed his kids were natural performers, but he and Russ should have started them off with something simpler and less rushed.

"Remember, we talked about make-believe?" Greg tugged on their hands to get their attention. They had only a few minutes left to film this shot. "In television and movies, we pretend. So we can tell a story and make people smile."

"Isn't that like lying?" Ben asked. "Mommy always tells us it's wrong to lie."

"No, we're not lying. We're acting."

"Do you catch your own fish, or are you acting?" Annie gazed straight at him.

"I catch my own fish."

"Then how come we can't?" Ben demanded.

"Well, we don't have time today. We're going to have to pretend you caught these."

"Greg." Russ held up his arm, his wristwatch facing out. "Let's get a move on."

"Okay, okay." Greg stood. "If you forget your lines," he instructed the kids, "don't worry. I'll help you."

"Hi, ya'll." A woman cut in front of Russ. She was waving Greg's book. "Will you autograph this for me? We're leaving right after the dinner."

"Excuse us," Russ grumbled.

"I won't be but a second." She pushed the book and a pen into Greg's hands and gazed fondly at Ben and Annie. "Are these your youngun's? Why, they're just adorable."

"If you wouldn't mind waiting, ma'am, I'll sign your book in a minute." Greg tried to hand the book back.

She didn't take it and beckoned another woman over. "This is my friend Mirabelle. We're huge fans of yours. Can the two of us get a picture with you?" She pulled a digital camera from her pocket and held it out to Russ. "Pretty please?"

"No. We're in the middle of filming."

"Oh, dear." She looked crushed.

"I promise." Greg gave her a tiny nudge. "I'll be right with you, and we'll get that picture."

Diminishing daylight and the approaching awards ceremony weren't their only pressing problems. Ben and Annie had become increasingly restless. To amuse themselves, they'd started playing a game of who could step on the other's toes the hardest. Ben was winning. In the process, Annie dropped her pole and fish.

"Kids, quiet down." Greg bent and retrieved the pole. He returned it to her.

"The fish is all dirty."

"No one will notice, honey."

"I want another fish."

"Greg," Russ intoned, hefting his camera off his shoulder for the fifth time.

"We can't get another fish, sweetie. This one will have to do."

"Give her my fish." A man stepped forward.

It was then Greg noticed the sizable audience that had formed around the insistent woman and her friend.

Swell. Just when he thought nothing else could go wrong.

"She can have mine," Ben said.

Grabbing the line, he swung his fish over his head and fired it at Annie, hitting her square in the neck. She screamed, danced in place and clawed at it, finally dislodging the fish. Her brother laughed.

"I hate you."

"Don't say things like that, Annie." Greg turned her toward him and saw she wasn't hurt, merely enraged.

"He's mean." Tears spilled down her beet-red cheeks.

"That was mean, Ben." Greg tried to ignore the noisy crowd and addressed his son. "Tell her you're sorry."

"Sorry," Ben muttered.

Greg rubbed his forehead. How often had he refereed fights between his children this summer? Did it ever get better?

He was beginning to think Corrine had a point.

"Damn it, Greg," Russ barked. "Do something."

"Maybe we should shoot this tomorrow."

"The tournament will be over tomorrow. We need this scene."

"Can you edit the background in?"

"Not without a lot of effort. Let's ditch the kids. Shoot the scene without them."

"Use my kids." A man pushed his boys forward. "They know how to listen."

The crowd broke into laughter at the man's joke. Greg didn't like it. Keeping calm was one thing. Allowing his children to behave like little hellions and walk all over him was another.

As if on cue, Ben picked up Annie's discarded fish and shoved it down the back of her shirt. She screeched and went into a frenzy. Wheeling on her twin, she pushed him to the ground. He fell like a ton of bricks, but came up again with the force of a linebacker.

Greg interceded, not a second too soon. "Hold it right there, buddy," he demanded, his voice gruff.

Ben didn't listen and took a swing at Annie, missing her chin by an inch.

Annie let loose with a high-pitched wail. "I'm telling Mommy."

Something inside Greg snapped. He heard the words pouring from his mouth, but it was as if someone else was speaking them. No, *yelling* them.

"That's enough!" he roared, and grabbed the children by their collars. "I've had it up to here with the pair of you. Quit your fighting this instant, you hear me?"

"She pushed me."

"He put a fish down my shirt."

Ben and Annie flung accusations at each other. Greg didn't care.

"You're both grounded. No horseback riding or swimming for the rest of the week."

"Daddy," Annie wailed.

"Not fair," whined Ben.

"Let's go." He began marching them toward the parking lot and his SUV.

"Greg," Russ called after him.

"Later." Greg wasn't sure what he was going to do with the kids once he got them back to their cabin, only that he had to remove them from the ever increasing and highly curious crowd.

"You can't leave now. The awards ceremony is coming up."

Greg hardly heard Russ through the drumming in his ears.

"Daddy, slow down." Annie pulled against him.

"I'm sick and tired of your constant fighting." He kept going. "You and your brother embarrassed me. And ruined the shoot."

It suddenly occurred to him how much he sounded like his father, and his feet froze.

Looking down, he saw two frightened faces staring up at him. Of course they were frightened. He'd never acted this way, and must seem like a stranger to them. Damn it. How could he be angry with them when hadn't spent enough time preparing them before putting them in front of the camera?

How could he be angry with Corrine for yelling when he was guilty of the same thing?

Boy, when he screwed up, he really screwed up.

"Guys, I'm sorry." He loosened his grip on them. "I shouldn't have gotten so mad at you."

Greg wasn't sure what he expected from them but it wasn't their frigid, silent stares.

"This tournament's been crazy." Everything the last two days had been crazy, starting with the fight with Corrine. He let go of Ben and Annie and placed his hands on their small heads, stroking their hair. "What do you say we go sit down for a second, just to cool off?"

"I want Mommy." Annie's lower lip trembled.

"You're a jerk," Ben said. He grabbed his sister's hand, and the two of them bolted into the crowd.

"Ben, Annie, come back here."

They were short in stature and the crowd was enormous. Greg quickly lost sight of them.

Agonizing pain filled his chest, nearly bringing him to his knees. This wasn't the first time his kids had taken off, but they hadn't been angry and confused and—this really hurt—despising him. He couldn't bear it if he lost everything he'd found with them this summer.

Or what he'd found with Corrine. She'd become a part of him, too. As had Bear Creek Ranch and her family.

He didn't want to leave. After the tournament, or ever.

While his first instinct was to tear through the hordes of people, looking for Ben and Annie, he listened to his head and ran to the main lodge. Natalie had assisted him in locating Ben and Annie before, and she'd do it again. After that, he'd drive back to the cabin on the chance they'd gone there.

With breath coming in bursts, he called Paulette and advised her of what she and Russ should do in his absence. Then, opening the door to the main lodge, he entered the lobby.

Natalie was surrounded by guests, but she took one look at him and hurried out from behind the counter. "What's wrong, Mr. Pfitser?"

GREG STOOD AT THE kitchen door, trying to think of what he'd say to Corrine. The phone call from Natalie telling him where the kids were had come in a few minutes ago. This was after a frantic and exhausting hour-and-fifteen-minute search. If the ranch wasn't overrun with guests and the employees scattered in a dozen different directions, Ben and Annie might have been found sooner.

Greg was just glad they were safe and sound.

They were also in the last place he'd expect them to be. Corrine's kitchen. He'd thought after what happened yesterday morning, they were just as angry at her as they were him. Apparently not.

He opened the door and went in. The noise was deafening. Dishes clattering, pots and pans clanging, staff calling orders and instructions back and forth. According to the clock on the wall, the dinner service was in full swing.

Because Greg would have missed the predinner awards ceremony, Paulette had taken charge and, working her incredible magic, arranged for the event to take place after dinner. He had, at most, a half hour before he had to get ready—and prepare a public apology to his fans. He owed them that much after his embarrassing display earlier.

"Great turnout today." Luke passed him, carrying trash. During the summer, Greg had gotten acquainted with most of the regular kitchen staff. "Heard reservations are going crazy."

"That's good."

"Yeah." Luke grinned. "Job security. Everybody's happy."

Greg, too. For Corrine and all the Tuckers.

"Can't wait to watch the shows. When are they on?"

"October, I think."

"Just in time for the holidays." Luke meandered toward the door, carting the trash bag over his shoulder like Santa Claus. "Oh, by the way, Corrine's in there."

"I was looking for my kids."

"Right." Luke whistled as he went out the door.

Greg traveled the short hall to the kitchen, nervous anticipation eating a hole in his stomach. At the entryway, he stopped to watch, marveling at how well the staff worked together in such a relatively cramped space.

A lot had gone through his mind since Ben and Annie ran

away from him, not all of it about his relationship with them and how he'd messed up. He'd also thought about Corrine and how unfair he'd been to her. She had every right not to speak to him again. He hoped she didn't exercise that right, at least not until he'd apologized and maybe slipped in something about his feelings for her.

He spotted Ben and Annie at last. He wouldn't have recognized them if not for hearing Annie's squeal—this one of delight. She and her brother stood at the sink, the same one he had the night he'd helped Corrine wash dishes. Ben and Annie were also washing dishes, if one could call it that. It looked like play to Greg. The staff didn't seem to mind the kids' presence, ducking beneath their arms, reaching over their heads and going around them if necessary.

Someone, he assumed Corrine, had given them stools to stand on and outfitted them in paper caps and white aprons that were far too big for their small bodies. The sink was filled to the brim with frothy suds and oversize pots and pans. Ben was using the sprayer like a water gun, drenching Annie. She didn't appear to mind, and at one point threw a handful of suds at him.

"Hey, you two, back to work. No horsing around on the job." Corrine appeared beside them.

Her order had been quietly delivered, yet firm. Greg waited for Ben and Annie to explode or rebel. It didn't happen. Instead, they muttered, "Okay," and returned to washing the pots and pans, though it still looked like playing. No matter; they were happy, content and, this was the most important part, behaving.

Corrine had pulled off the impossible. She was nothing short of amazing.

And he was crazy, madly in love with her.

To hell with both of them being stuck in the past. It was

time to move on, and he didn't want to make the journey alone. Now, he need only convince Corrine to join him.

Greg was still watching the three people who mattered most in the world to him when Gerrie passed by, carrying a crate of apples on her way to the walk-in cooler. "How's it going, Mr. Pfitser?"

At the sound of his name, Corrine, Ben and Annie all turned to look at him. Before Greg could wonder if the kids had gotten over being angry at him, they jumped off their stools and ran straight toward him, flinging their arms around his waist.

Step one accomplished, and it was a good one. He closed his eyes and returned their hug, holding them as tightly as possible without crushing them.

"Daddy." Annie beamed up at him. "I'm so glad you're here."

"Me, too." His voice cracked.

"We're working for Corrine," Ben said proudly.

"I see that."

"She told us if we do a good job, she's going to give us some ice cream. Do you want some ice cream, too?"

"Do I have to wash dishes?"

"Of course," Corrine said, walking toward them, a smile pulling at the corners of her lips.

Did this mean she wasn't angry at him, either?

"Thank you for everything you've done for the ranch," she said. "We're very grateful."

"No, thank *you*." He let go of the kids to meet her halfway.

"For what?"

"Teaching me that I'm not my father, and a little reasonable discipline now and again is a good thing."

"So is kicking back and taking it easy. Within reason," she added with a laugh.

Greg took the plunge. "I'm sorry about yesterday morning. I was wrong."

"Me, too."

"I can't believe I got mad at you for yelling at Ben and Annie. Not after the display I put on today." He patted Ben's and Annie's heads. "I surprised they're even talking to me."

"Are you kidding? They adore you."

"What about their boss?"

"Me?" She pointed to herself.

"Yes."

All at once, the entire kitchen went quiet. Every pair of eyes, including those of his kids, were focused on him and Corrine.

She hesitated. Greg thought the wait was going to kill him but he didn't dare rush her. Didn't dare move.

"I've been afraid a long time."

"Are you still?"

"Yes. That you're going to leave without me telling you how I really feel."

Greg might have made the first move, but it was Corrine who flew into his arms. Paying no attention to their audience, or their whoops and hollers, he kissed her fiercely, possessively, as if they hadn't been apart for days and wouldn't be ever again if he had any say in the matter.

Annie's tug on his pant leg distracted him.

"Daddy, are we going to live at Bear Creek Ranch now?"

"I don't know. Maybe not on the ranch, but near it. So we can come here all the time when you and your brother visit me. Us," he corrected, and looked to Corrine for confirmation.

"What about buying a house in Denver to be near the kids?"

"As much as I travel, I can always fit a quick trip in to see them. And there's always the summer and next year's tournament." He groaned and clamped a hand to the side of his head. "The tournament! I have to get out there. I left Russ and Paulette with a pretty big mess." He'd be lucky if his crew still talked to him, much less still worked for him. "Kids, why don't you come with me."

"Wait!" Corrine stood back and evaluated all three of them. "There are a couple of conditions." She tried to come across as serious. Greg doubted anyone was fooled. "You and the kids have to learn to pick up after yourselves and pitch in with the housework. And Belle must be trained to leave the garbage alone."

"I'll do the dishes," Ben offered.

"An excellent start."

Greg studied her in return. "I have my own conditions, too."

"Oh?" She raised her brows.

"You have to promise to dedicate at least one day a week to nothing but fun and relaxation."

"I see." She folded her arms across her middle, appearing to deliberate. "You drive a hard bargain, Mr. Pfitser." Unable to maintain the charade, she broke into a sunny smile that lit up the room as it washed over him. "But I think that's an arrangement I can live with."

He pulled her into another embrace, one that included Ben and Annie. "For how long?"

Corrine lifted her mouth to his and said against his lips, "How does forever and ever sound to you?"

* * * * *

Watch for Cathy McDavid's next story set on Bear Creek Ranch—it's cousin Carolina's turn to find love in THE ACCIDENTAL SHERIFF. Coming May 2010 only from Harlequin American Romance.

Rancher Ramsey Westmoreland's temporary cook is way too attractive for his liking. Little does he know Chloe Burton came to his ranch with another agenda entirely....

That man across the street had to be, without a doubt, the most handsome man she'd ever seen.

Chloe Burton's pulse beat rhythmically as he stopped to talk to another man in front of a feed store. He was tall, dark and every inch of sexy—from his Stetson to the well-worn leather boots on his feet. And from the way his jeans and Western shirt fit his broad muscular shoulders, it was quite obvious he had everything it took to separate the men from the boys. The combination was enough to corrupt any woman's mind and had her weakening even from a distance. Her body felt flushed. It was hot. Unsettled.

Over the past year the only male who had gotten her time and attention had been the e-mail. That was simply pathetic, especially since now she was practically drooling simply at the sight of a man. Even his stance—both hands in his jeans pockets, legs braced apart, was a pose she would carry to her dreams.

And he was smiling, evidently enjoying the conversation being exchanged. He had dimples, incredibly sexy dimples in not one but both cheeks.

"What are you staring at, Clo?"

Chloe nearly jumped. She'd forgotten she had a lunch date. She glanced over the table at her best friend from college, Lucia Conyers.

"Take a look at that man across the street in the blue shirt, Lucia. Will he not be perfect for Denver's first issue of *Simply Irresistible* or what?" Chloe asked with so much excitement she almost couldn't stand it.

She was the owner of *Simply Irresistible*, a magazine for today's up-and-coming woman. Their once-a-year Irresistible Man cover, which highlighted a man the magazine felt deserved the honor, had increased sales enough for Chloe to open a Denver office.

When Lucia didn't say anything but kept staring, Chloe's smile widened. "Well?"

Lucia glanced across the booth at her. "Since you asked, I'll tell you what I see. One of the Westmorelands—Ramsey Westmoreland. And yes, he'd be perfect for the cover, but he won't do it."

Chloe raised a brow. "He'd get paid for his services, of course."

Lucia laughed and shook her head. "Getting paid won't be the issue, Clo—Ramsey is one of the wealthiest sheep ranchers in this part of Colorado. But everyone knows what a private person he is. Trust me—he won't do it."

Chloe couldn't help but smile. The man was the epitome of what she was looking for in a magazine cover and she was determined that whatever it took, he would be it.

"Umm, I don't like that look on your face, Chloe. I've seen it before and know exactly what it means."

She watched as Ramsey Westmoreland entered the store with a swagger that made her almost breathless. She *would* be seeing him again.

Look for Silhouette Desire's
HOT WESTMORELAND NIGHTS by Brenda Jackson,
available March 9 wherever books are sold.

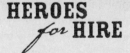

Devastating, dark-hearted and...
looking for brides.

Look for

BOUGHT:
DESTITUTE YET DEFIANT

by *Sarah Morgan*

#2902

From the lowliest slums to Millionaire's Row...
these men have everything now but their brides—
and they'll settle for nothing less than the best!

Available March 2010
from Harlequin Presents!

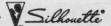

SPECIAL EDITION

FROM *USA TODAY* BESTSELLING AUTHOR
CHRISTINE RIMMER

A BRIDE FOR
JERICHO BRAVO

Marnie Jones had long ago buried her wild-child
impulses and opted to be "safe," romantically
speaking. But one look at born rebel Jericho Bravo
and she began to wonder if her thrill-seeking side
was about to be revived. Because if ever there was
a man worth taking a chance on, there he was,
right within her grasp....

Available in March
wherever books are sold.

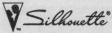

ROMANTIC
SUSPENSE

Sparked by Danger, Fueled by Passion.

Introducing a brand-new miniseries
Lawmen of Black Rock

Peyton Wilkerson's life shatters when her
four-month-old daughter, Lilly, vanishes.
But handsome sheriff Tom Grayson is
determined to put the pieces together and
reunite her with her baby. Will Tom be able
to protect Peyton and Lilly while fighting
his own growing feelings?

Find out in
His Case, Her Baby
by
CARLA CASSIDY

Available in March wherever books are sold

REQUEST YOUR FREE BOOKS!

2 FREE NOVELS PLUS 2 FREE GIFTS!

HARLEQUIN®

American ★ Romance®

Love, Home & Happiness!

YES! Please send me 2 FREE Harlequin® American Romance® novels and my 2 FREE gifts (gifts are worth about $10). After receiving them, if I don't wish to receive any more books, I can return the shipping statement marked "cancel." If I don't cancel, I will receive 4 brand-new novels every month and be billed just $4.24 per book in the U.S. or $4.99 per book in Canada. That's a saving of close to 15% off the cover price! It's quite a bargain! Shipping and handling is just 50¢ per book in the U.S. and 75¢ per book in Canada.* I understand that accepting the 2 free books and gifts places me under no obligation to buy anything. I can always return a shipment and cancel at any time. Even if I never buy another book from Harlequin, the two free books and gifts are mine to keep forever.

154 HDN E4CC   354 HDN E4CN

Name	(PLEASE PRINT)	
Address		Apt. #
City	State/Prov.	Zip/Postal Code

Signature (if under 18, a parent or guardian must sign)

Mail to the **Harlequin Reader Service:**
IN U.S.A.: P.O. Box 1867, Buffalo, NY 14240-1867
IN CANADA: P.O. Box 609, Fort Erie, Ontario L2A 5X3

Not valid for current subscribers to Harlequin® American Romance® books.

Want to try two free books from another line?
Call 1-800-873-8635 or visit www.morefreebooks.com.

* Terms and prices subject to change without notice. Prices do not include applicable taxes. N.Y. residents add applicable sales tax. Canadian residents will be charged applicable provincial taxes and GST. Offer not valid in Quebec. This offer is limited to one order per household. All orders subject to approval. Credit or debit balances in a customer's account(s) may be offset by any other outstanding balance owed by or to the customer. Please allow 4 to 6 weeks for delivery. Offer available while quantities last.

Your Privacy: Harlequin is committed to protecting your privacy. Our Privacy Policy is available online at www.eHarlequin.com or upon request from the Reader Service. From time to time we make our lists of customers available to reputable third parties who may have a product or service of interest to you. If you would prefer we not share your name and address, please check here. ☐

Help us get it right—We strive for accurate, respectful and relevant communications. To clarify or modify your communication preferences, visit us at www.ReaderService.com/consumerschoice.

HARI0

THE WESTMORELANDS

NEW YORK TIMES
bestselling author

BRENDA JACKSON

HOT WESTMORELAND NIGHTS

Ramsey Westmoreland knew better than to lust after the hired help. But Chloe, the new cook, was just so delectable. Though their affair was growing steamier, Chloe's motives became suspicious. And when he learned Chloe was carrying his child this Westmoreland Rancher had to choose between pride or duty.

Available March 2010 wherever books are sold.

Always Powerful, Passionate and Provocative.